"Wake up, Chastity."

Sin leaned forward and pressed his lips to hers, letting her sweet taste melt on his mouth.

Her eyelashes fluttered and her eyes opened halfway, in that twilight between sleep and wakefulness. "I was dreaming about you," she whispered. "And here you are."

Sin ran his fingertips over her lips. "I couldn't stay away."

She opened her mouth and sucked on his fingertip—a move that Sin felt deep in his gut—then lifted her arms and circled his neck. Pulling him down to her, she said, "Take me."

There were no more words. They needed none. Only the sound of heavy breathing broke the stillness as they tore off their clothing and melded their bodies together.

Sin had never experienced a pleasure so intense as they both found their release.

Eventually, gradually, their breathing slowed to something approaching normal and he lifted his head to gently kiss Chastity's cheek.

"That wasn't a dream," she murmured.

Sin smiled down at her as her eyes drifted closed. "Oh, yes, it was, darlin'."

Meg Lacey first discovered romance in the sixth grade when she wrote her own version of *Gone with the Wind.* However, her writing career didn't last. Instead, she went into theater, earned her degree and finally ended up in television as a writer-producer. Currently, she is president of Parke Media, a TV and multimedia production company in Cincinnati, Ohio. Over the years, she has also been an actress, director, copywriter, creative dramatics teacher, mime, mom, college instructor and school bus driver. "Boy," she says of the last, "there are stories in that experience."

Sexy As Sin came about after Meg read an article in the newspaper that said the local Renaissance Festival was getting so many requests for weddings that they built a chapel on the festival grounds and hired a wedding planner. That got her writer's mind whirling. What would happen if a well-behaved professor, Chastity Goodwin, whose passion was the past, collided with bad boy Sin O'Connor, a man focused on reshaping the future via computer programming?

We hope you enjoy finding out in this fun and sexy story of opposites who attract! And watch for Meg Lacey's next book, *Make Me Over,* coming in November 1999 from Harlequin Duets.

SEXY AS SIN
Meg Lacey

HARLEQUIN®

TORONTO • NEW YORK • LONDON
AMSTERDAM • PARIS • SYDNEY • HAMBURG
STOCKHOLM • ATHENS • TOKYO • MILAN • MADRID
PRAGUE • WARSAW • BUDAPEST • AUCKLAND

For Guy

ISBN 0-373-25834-8

SEXY AS SIN

CHASTITY GOODWIN GLANCED toward the window behind the antique writing desk, expecting to see her very late appointment come dashing up the street like a white knight riding a charger.

At the moment, however, the street was empty.

"Where is the best man?" she muttered as she flipped the pages of her Day-Timer organizer to confirm she'd not made a scheduling error. Looking up from the detailed pages that neatly catalogued each day of her life, Chastity checked the delicate gold watch encircling her wrist and sighed. *Two-thirty.* She rubbed her forehead. Obviously he wasn't coming this time, either.

Today would make the third appointment he'd missed. If he didn't show up soon, he'd be going to the wedding in his birthday suit. Chastity grinned as she imagined the wedding guests' reactions. Even at a Renaissance Festival wedding, where the attire of the guests ranged from bishops to court ladies to jailers to jesters, a best man as naked as the day he was born would cause some comment.

Especially in Gloriana, New York.

Chastity placed her appointment book on the elegant desk and walked closer to the mullion-paned window and glanced out. Still no sign of activity, foreign or otherwise, disturbed the midday quiet of the old neighborhood. Here, life moved at its accustomed pace as the summer weather zapped the energy level of her many elderly neighbors, keeping them inside to nap through the steamy July afternoon. She cast another glance up and down the silent street. Same as usual. Chastity had to admit that sameness was one of the things she liked about the small town—its serenity and lack of surprises. There was a sense of history here, of continuity.

She started to turn away from the window when a loud hum, like the angry buzzing of bees caught her attention. Pulling back the lace curtain, she peered outside and gasped. A big, black motorcycle roared down the street, looking for all the world like the chariot to hell. The bike skidded to a stop in front of her house and abruptly quieted, leaving the aggressive echo of the engine's noise behind, still breaking the silence. The man astride the bike glanced quickly at her house, then swung his leg over the black metal monster to set foot on the sidewalk.

Startled at the sight of this unexpected visitor, Chastity leaned closer to the window until her nose touched the glass. If the bike was the chariot to hell, surely the man riding it was the perfect driver. Even in the heat, he was dressed all in black—black leather jacket, black jeans, black boots. Only a hint of white was visible at his throat, a T-shirt perhaps? As he swooped down upon her sidewalk like a huge bird of prey, Chastity suddenly regretted the solitude of the peaceful neighborhood.

She stepped back from the window and wondered what to do when the bell rang. It was an impatient ring, as if the ringer had little time to waste on manners. Biting her lip, she darted a glance toward her appointment book.

The best man? No. This guy couldn't possibly be Harrison O'Connor's brother...not Harrison of the infinitely polite manners. Harrison was the kind of man who would apologize smoothly to a mugger for not carrying enough money. No, this couldn't be Harrison's brother.

So who was he?

With a deep breath, Chastity turned to face the hallway. She exhaled and forced herself to move. Stomach churning, she carefully put one foot in front of the other and walked to the door. She pulled it ajar, taking care to open it only far enough for conversation.

The man upon her porch stood insolently, knee cocked, hip outthrust, and looked her over. "I'm Sin," he said.

Chastity grabbed her throat. "Of course you are," she said, so taken aback by his announcement that her voice barely whispered through the air to reach his ears. It had finally happened. All those years of studying medieval literature had driven her mad!

"Sin O'Connor."

"Sin...O'Connor?" Had Harrison even mentioned his brother's name? This wedding was happening so fast, Chastity wasn't sure.

Impatiently, Sin thrust one hand through his black hair, smoothing back the wayward lock falling onto his brow. "I've got an appointment for two o'clock."

Chastity stared at him, taking in his bad-boy good looks, which reminded her of the newest actor playing Agent 007 at the movies. Her eyes lingered on the collar-length, black hair blown back by the wind, except for one thick lock that slashed over his forehead. With a sense of shock, she met the heat of his golden eyes as they bored into her. Except for her black cat, Squash, she'd never seen eyes that color before. Chastity couldn't remember having made a date with the devil. And this guy had the look of him...all fire and seduction. *Lord help me.* One look at him and she started thinking of scarlet sheets and strawberries dipped in rich, dark chocolate.

Fingers snapped under her nose. "Hello in there."

Chastity fought her way back to the present. "Pardon?"

"You're not sleepwalking are you?"

That brought her to her senses. "No. Of course not."

He leaned his tall body against the doorjamb, seeming all of a sudden ready to enjoy himself. "That's good. I'm not used to women going to sleep on me."

Chastity's lips trembled as she tried to dispel the sudden disturbing image of the two of them in bed. *I'll just bet you aren't.*

He smiled and lifted a brow. "Do I have the right house? I'm looking for a wedding planner."

Reeling under the blinding wattage of his smile, a slash of white in his tanned face, Chastity forced herself to gather her brain cells together one by one so she could answer coherently, "You…um…you've found one."

His smile broadened. "Good."

It was the satisfaction in that smile that finally pulled her together. As if he not only knew his impact on women, but took it for granted. That got her dander up. She checked her watch and forced a cool statement through her lips. "However, Mr. O'Connor, you're late."

"Yeah. I'm sorry about that. I got this idea on the way here, and had to stop to get it down. It was important."

"More important than your brother's wedding?"

Sin laughed and rested his arm against the doorjamb. "Oh, much. My brother's wedding will only touch two people. This idea will touch millions of lives from now until the next millennium."

Chastity stared at him, both repelled and attracted

by the snapping light in his eyes. "The *next* millennium? I don't like to think that far into the future myself. It seems so cold and distant."

A shocked expression exploded onto Sin's face. "The future isn't distant. The future is now."

At that statement, Chastity opened the door wide and indicated he come inside. "That's right, Mr. O'Connor. To me the future is your brother's wedding in five days. Now if you don't mind, I'd like to get started."

Sin checked his watch, then said, "Fine. I can only spare a few minutes, though. So whaddaya say we get this over with. I need to get on with some work."

Chastity bristled as he stepped past her into the hallway. He walked purposefully, as if he had somewhere important to go and the world had better get out of his way. The easy arrogance of his movement and the leashed grace of his physique made her breath come faster once again. She shook her head. What on earth was the matter with her? She didn't like know-it-all arrogant men with aggressive opinions. She knew she shouldn't say anything, but she couldn't help it.

"Obviously we'd have more than a few minutes if you had been here on time."

"Ah, back to that are we?" He stopped and turned so abruptly that Chastity slammed into him. She gasped as his arms automatically went around her to stop them from overbalancing. Her nose was instantly buried in his T-shirt. She could smell him, all tangy male with a faint tinge of the fresh outdoors from riding his motorcycle...at breakneck speed, she'd bet. Because suddenly Chastity wanted to stay right where she was, she jerked herself upright and stepped back.

"Are you always so obsessed with time?" Sin continued.

Chastity could feel her mouth opening and closing

like a beached fish. No one had ever asked her that before. In today's world, who wasn't? Time was the only thing people didn't possess in abundance. "Only when it's not being used to my advantage."

Sin chuckled, then wrinkled his brow as he stared at her curiously. "Don't you ever want to go off on a tangent and explore something new without ever thinking of how long it'll take?"

"Well, of course I do. I'm a historian. We live for that sort of thing. You should see me in a library."

"I thought you were a wedding planner."

"Only in the summer, during the Renaissance Festival." Because she could see him gearing up to continue his questioning, she interrupted. "Excuse me, I don't mean to be rude—"

"Oh, I think you should always *mean* to be rude. Or, why do it?" He grinned down at her. "It seems such a waste of time otherwise...all that apologizing."

Chastity suddenly felt like Alice after falling down the rabbit hole. She wondered how she'd so completely lost all control of the situation. "Mr...."

"Sin."

Exasperated, Chastity exhaled, blowing the annoying, curly tendrils of her hair away from her forehead. "Look, I don't care if your name is Mordred—"

"I sure would."

Intrigued by his smile, but having none of his charm, Chastity gritted her teeth and forced her words between them. " I have twenty trillion things to do this afternoon and I'm behind. So we must fit this costume on your *very late* body immediately." She swept by him in as grand a fashion as she could manage, almost slipping on the scatter rug inside the sitting room archway.

Sin reached for her arm, but released it at first touch as she grabbed at the molding on the doorway. "Whatever you say, Miss..."

"Ms." she snapped.

"Wouldn't that actually be mistress, in Renaissance terms?"

Chastity jerked. How odd that he'd know the correct terminology for addressing a single woman in olden times. Then, she realized, he was just the sort of man to mention the word *mistress* in a casual conversation with a complete stranger. She sent him a narrow glance over her shoulder. This man was able to wind her up faster than anyone she'd ever met. Chastity couldn't understand it. She'd always thought herself so even-tempered. "Mistress would be correct terminology, however—"

"Ms. will do?"

Chastity tried her hardest to keep a straight face, but couldn't manage it. She smiled. "I give up. Please, since you're Harrison's brother, call me Chastity."

Sin positively recoiled. "Chastity?"

"Chastity Goodwin."

Sin laughed. "You're kidding me, right?"

"Absolutely not. What's so funny?"

He stared at her for a moment, taking his time, allowing his eyes to travel slowly from her head to her feet, making sure he spent plenty of time on the places in between. "The name fits."

Right about then Chastity would have given her entire collection of leather-bound Shakespeare for a frying pan big enough and heavy enough to make this arrogant oaf see stars for eternity! Or longer.

Sin must have read her expression because he held up his hands, in a conciliatory gesture. "I meant that as a compliment."

Chastity wished she could have reverted to a display of childish temper, but manners won out. She thought a great deal of manners. "Perhaps we should drop the subject."

"That might be rather difficult. I still have to call you something."

She watched him chewing over the problem, amazed at his total absorption. Now she could understand how he would happily stop by the side of the road to note an idea when it struck, why time didn't seem to concern him. Studying his perplexed face, Chastity finally felt as if she were getting the upper hand in this strange conversation, which made her a lot happier. "You have two choices as I see it—Chastity or Ms. Goodwin. Take your pick."

"No can do." His golden gaze lifted from contemplation of his black boots and rammed head on into hers. "Don't worry. I'll come up with something."

"I don't want you to come up with something. I am perfectly happy with my name and I don't—"

"Excuse me," Sin looked at his watch. "I really think we should do something about my tuxedo, don't you?"

Cut off just as she was finding the right words to deflate the cocky devil who'd invaded her life, Chastity stared at him. "What tuxedo?"

He gave her a strange look. "The one for the wedding. I'm here for a fitting. That's what we've been talking about."

Chastity folded her arms, trying to keep the satisfaction from her voice as it was very apparent this man wouldn't take kindly to what she was going to say. "Actually, you don't have to wear a tuxedo."

"Great. I don't mind telling you I was going to wear it under protest. The only outfit I feel comfortable in is jeans and a shirt. It's what I always wear. They just fit right, sort of mold to the body. You know what I'm saying?"

"A close fit is important to you, is it?"

He looked surprised. "Yeah. I guess it is."

Chastity rubbed her hands together. "I've got just the thing for you. You're going to love this."

"I am?"

"Trust me. Let's go back to my studio and I'll show you, okay?"

"Sure." He checked his watch. "I'm at your disposal for about twenty more minutes, then I'm outta here. I'm expecting a phone call from overseas."

"Oh, I think twenty minutes will do it." Chastity led the way through the old-fashioned parlor until she reached a set of double doors. She slid one of them back onto the track that disappeared into the thick, old-fashioned brick wall. Then she stepped inside her studio. It was here that she felt truly productive. Here with her desk and computer tucked in one corner and her books lining all of the walls around the room. In another corner, standing in the north light was an artist's easel; simple sketches were taped or tacked up all over the board. Another corner of the room was dominated by a large worktable and a sewing machine, with a mirror and hanging rack standing nearby. However, what made the room unique were the six mannequins dressed in costumes at various stages of completion.

The group of men and women stood as if attending a party on a summer afternoon. The gleam of satin and the sheen of silk shimmered in the ever-changing patterns of sunlight as the breeze stirred the leaves of the old elm outside the windows.

Chastity walked by one of the dummies and couldn't help but touch the drooping lace of the glorious yellow bridal gown. Sometimes the mannequins seemed alive to her, although she would never admit it to anyone. She waved at the figures, saying over her shoulder to Sin, "Meet the wedding party."

She glanced behind her to see Sin dumbstruck in the

middle of the room as he stared at the half-dressed silhouettes.

"What did you do, loot a department store window?"

Chastity laughed. "No. Last year, one of the old clothing stores downtown was going out of business. The owner mentioned it to my dad. Since I'd just started working with the wedding costumes at that point and needed something to fit the patterns onto, I rushed down and picked them up." She glanced fondly at them. To Chastity, they took on new personalities every time she dressed them for a wedding.

"It's like living with your own mob."

"There are only six of them." Chastity shrugged. "Besides, I like crowds."

Sin shuddered. "I hate them." He eyed the group again. "Besides that, what happens when you wander down here in the middle of the night? I'd think they'd scare the hell out of you."

"First of all, I don't wander in the middle of the night. I'm a very sound sleeper. Second of all, I know they're here, so I'm expecting to see them. Ergo—they wouldn't surprise me at all."

"Ergo? Who in this century says *ergo*?"

Chastity could feel her face heat with annoyance. She forced herself to count to ten. "Any scholar worth her salt can say *ergo* because any scholar worth her salt knows what it means."

Sin draped his arm over the mannequin standing next to him. "Well, I know what it means, too, don't you old man? *Therefore* I sure as hell wouldn't run around saying it to a perfect stranger. Think of the odd impression you might give me."

"I don't care what type of impression I give you. I don't even know you. And from what I've seen so far—Harrison's brother or not—I don't care if I get to know you any better than I do right now."

He sent her a satisfied smile and stepped away from the mannequin, glancing back at the frozen figure for confirmation. "Now that was definitely rude." He lifted one finely shaped black eyebrow as he looked back to Chastity. "I'll bet you meant it to be, didn't you?"

Stunned by the complete lack of courtesy she'd just shown him, Chastity took a deep breath to apologize, then changed her mind. "I most certainly did," she muttered defiantly.

"Now we're getting somewhere."

"What do you mean?"

He peeled off his leather jacket. "Well, I can't possibly kiss you if you're going to starch up all the time. It'll put me off my game."

"I don't want you to kiss me at all!"

"Okay, then I'll forget it. Just let me see my wedding duds and I'll be off."

Still trying to recover from his unexpected statement about kissing, and rather perturbed that she had found it somewhat interesting, she said, "You're standing next to part of it."

"What? Not this thing on my man here?" After squinting at it for a moment, he backed up for a better look.

Chastity stared at the rich maroon-and-gilt doublet she'd pinned in place on the mannequin that morning. "Well, that's not all of it."

Scowling, Sin looked down. "I hope not. There aren't any pants. Not that I'm going to wear the glittery-looking top, either." He pointed an emphatic finger in her direction. "But, pants...I gotta have pants."

"You're not wearing pants."

"What do you mean, I'm not wearing pants? I can't go racing around in my jockstrap, you know."

"Oh, my." She blinked, wishing she could fan away the hot image Sin O'Connor had suddenly dropped into her mind. An image far removed from the historical ones with which she was comfortable. "You, um, you won't need that sort of thing. I've got something else for...uh..." She coughed delicately, knowing she was bright scarlet and unable to do a thing about it. "For support. But I need to take your measurements to make sure everything will fit. I try to stay very historically accurate so it'll look strange if it's too baggy."

"If what's baggy?"

"Your pants, of course."

"You just said I'm not wearing pants."

"Not pants the way you think of pants. But if the fit is baggy and droopy, then the bottom of the outfit looks odd."

"Except for the first time my mom slapped diapers on me," Sin said, with a dangerous look, "no woman has *ever* called my bottom baggy."

Chastity ignored this statement. It wasn't hard for her to read the provocative look he gave her. Obviously he was just waiting for a chance to take off. Well, she had news for him. She wasn't going to give it to him. Instead, she was going to get this job done first, then get this annoying man out of here—if it killed her. *And it probably would.* Reaching toward the table, she yanked a long measuring tape from under a pile of lace. Then she stepped toward the dressing mirror and the hanging rack. "Would you mind coming over here so I can do a double check before I give them to you to try on."

She bit back a chuckle as he trod across the room toward her. You would have thought her tape measure was a bullwhip from his approach. He stopped close to the mirror, leaving her enough room to stand directly in front of it. "I tried to use your brother for a guide but—"

"Then you don't really need me to—"

"He said he was a bit taller, so I do need to make sure—" She lifted her skirt a bit and dropped to her knees in front of him, which brought her face to eye level with his hips.

"What the hell are you doing?"

Suddenly that was exactly what she was asking herself as she stared at the slim masculine body, tightly encased in soft black jeans. She tried not to focus on his most interesting angle, jerking her stare to the side of his hip instead. "Re-research," she stammered as she said the word. "I mean measurements, not re—Taking your measurements." Her position certainly wasn't conducive to dignity, and definitely not to scholarly research, come to that. Gingerly she extended the tape to the outside of his hips and measured from his waist to his ankle. She kept her eyes firmly on the numbers, afraid if she glanced anywhere else she'd be unable to finish the job. That didn't stop her from wanting to blow on her fingers to cool them off, though. She was all too aware of the heat of his body as she pressed the tape against him.

Idiot. You've done this with any number of people. It's no different with this man.

But that wasn't strictly true. She wasn't sure why this was different. Maybe it was because, for the first time, she had more interest in the inside leg measurement than the outside. She'd never met a man like this in her entire life. Her taste tended to run to the familiar—to the academic and overly well-bred men she could control. Those who were more turned on by their next research article than by the woman by their side. No, Chastity had never been attracted to the sort of

man who seemed to know more about sin than even
his name implied. Until now of course. As she stared at
the rock-hard muscles in front of her and imagined
their strength, she was suddenly aware of what she'd
been missing.

Chastity felt her face burst into flame. Her hand
trembled as she toyed with the tape measure. The
room was so silent she could hear a stray dove cooing
under the eaves of the old house. The clock on her desk
clicked, changing minutes so loudly it sounded like
thunder to her. In slow motion, it seemed, her hand
moved to the inside of his thigh. Hesitantly she took
the head of the tape measure and raised it higher, trying to keep her breathing under control as she approached the target.

That's when she made a big mistake. Her eyes jerked
upward and collided with his burning gold gaze. She
was unable to look away. His eyes widened, then narrowed abruptly to consider her.

She didn't understand what was happening. This
man was a stranger to her. She couldn't remember having felt this awareness, this anticipation, this longing
before. Not even with Jeremy, the man she'd been dating for some time. They had an understanding...of
sorts. At the moment, however, she couldn't exactly remember what they'd understood. How odd!

Chastity studied the exciting face above her, her
imagination caught by the stubbly beard that lightly
shadowed the bold line of his jaw and framed his firm
lips. *What would that feel like against my skin?* Would it
be as rough as Squash's cat's tongue? Or would his
beard have a different effect? Would it make her nerves
jump as much as they were jumping now?

One of us better exhale before we both keel over, she
thought frantically. The image of both of them slump-
ing down, then tangling on the floor together, didn't

help her ability to breathe at all. Instead her vision blurred, making Sin O'Connor's golden gaze expand until it filled the universe. Finally, Chastity gasped, gulping in air like a greedy glutton. Her mind worked at top speed. Searching for an explanation, she decided the faintness was probably hunger. She hadn't eaten lunch, had she? That was it. Low blood sugar. The obvious source for her odd reaction.

"I'm hungry."

Oh, my God, I didn't say that aloud, did I?

Judging by the look on his face, she had. She felt his hands drop onto her shoulders. His fingers tightened. She couldn't move. Her nerves started to leap in all directions, her blood pounded like jungle drums in her ears, her temperature hit the skylight, her stomach rumbled then clenched and—

"*Hic!*" The sound bounced off the mirror behind them and seemed to ricochet around the room.

Damn and blast it to hell and beyond! I've got the hiccups.

Chastity thought she'd outgrown that childish nervous habit. Obviously not. She tried to take a deep breath to control the noisy spasms, but instead let out a rapid-fire series of hiccups.

"Hic...hic...hic..."

The sound didn't register as Sin tried to tear his gaze from hers, wondering what the hell was going on. *This long-haired, redheaded witch was casting some kind of spell over him.*

He could almost feel his blood racing downhill to bring his unexplained desire to life. Unexplained because this wasn't the type of woman who ordinarily attracted him. But if he wasn't attracted to her, why was his body straining against his clothes? Why were his hands burning as he shaped her shoulders under his fingertips?

Why did he feel as if he were falling into this woman's wide blue eyes? Eyes so blue they put the sky to shame. Confused, he finally tore his gaze from hers. Trying to subdue his rising passion, he forced himself to think of something else. He cast about frantically for something else to focus on—the square root of eighty-four, the code he was working on for the new software he was developing—anything. Anything so he could put the brakes on his passion before it embarrassed both of them. But his gaze came back to lock onto hers.

Just when he despaired of thinking about anything beyond how much he wanted to nuzzle the soft rose of her skin where the tender curve of her neck met her sweet shoulder, or how much he wanted to cup her chin with his hand and crush her strawberry-tinted, full lips under his own, he became aware of the sound.

"*Hic. Hic*...oh, damn—*hic, hic*—it!"

Rescued by an unlikely source, his passion declined as rapidly as it had risen. Startled, Sin let out the breath he'd been holding and refocused on Chastity.

Hiccups? From this elegant woman with the swanlike grace? Sin's lips trembled as he tried to keep a straight face. Studying her mortified expression, Sin decided that God either had a sense of decorum, or a great sense of humor. Why else would hiccups strike without warning like this?

"Bless you," he said. "No wait a minute, that's for a sneeze isn't it?" He rubbed his chin. "What do you say for hiccups?"

"You don't—*hic*—say anything for hic—c-*cups*. Oh lord." Chastity Goodwin sat back on her heels and hid her face with both hands. The tape measure she'd been using trailed between her fingers.

Sin squatted in front of her and pulled her hands away from her face. "I think one rescue a day is about all you can expect from him, sweetheart."

Chastity's head jerked up. "Don't call me sweetheart. *Hic!* I don't know you well enough for you to be that free with your endearments."

"With my endearments? You talk like a textbook."

"I do not!"

"Look, I already told you. I can't call you Chastity, or even Ms. Goodwin."

"Very well, then you can call me Dr. Goodwin."

Puzzled, Sin stared at her. "You're a doctor? First you're a wedding planner, then you tell me you're a scholar. What's next? A nuclear physicist?"

Chastity shuddered. "Ohhh, no. I wouldn't be suited for that at all." She stopped and considered, her face flushed. The tape measure lay discarded in her lap as she waved her hands to help express her thoughts. "Although I do admire the thought of that profession in a way...the curiosity of trying to break down matter into its smallest elements. However, I firmly believe it's because of man's insatiable appetite for trying to change the entire world around him—and not always for the better I might add—that the world around him is in the shape it's in."

He squatted before her, clasped his hands, lacing the fingers together and murmured provocatively, "The world is in the shape it's in because people are not moving fast enough to make the future and all of its possibilities a reality today." Sin had never met a woman so contrary—cool water on the outside, but liquid fire on the inside, he'd bet. She was so appealing when she let herself go, he couldn't help adding more fuel to the fire. "The problem is, people are stuck in the way things used to be done—bogged down in old 'historical' systems that are completely outmoded."

"I don't believe that at all. How can you put the blame on history? If it weren't for history you would have no insight into the mistakes that had been made or the achievements that have been left to continue—"

"Doctor." Sin snapped his fingers as realization dawned. "Did you recently get your Ph.D.?"

"*Hic.* Now that you mention it, I did."

Sin nodded, then grinned. "I thought so. You can always tell a new Ph.D. by the pedantic arguments they put forth at the drop of a hat."

"Pedantic! I'll have you know, my degree is in the literature and arts of the Renaissance. It wasn't pedantic. It was energetic. It was a time of great intellectual flowering and the enthusiastic embracement of all knowledge and learning."

"Unfortunately, it was also about three or four centuries ago."

"What does that have to do with anything?"

"Nothing. That's my point."

"How...*hic*...how can you say that?"

"Read my lips, Doc. If society doesn't focus on where it's going and get there as rapidly as possible, then—" He stopped, tilted his head and considered her expressive eyes, which were snapping with life as he spoke. "Doc. Hey, I like that. I'll call you Doc."

"*That* is the most annoying nickname I can think of. I could never consider allowing anyone to call me Doc. It makes me feel like a character in a sitcom! Or a character in that computer game they keep advertising on television. The one where the mad scientist asks you to open the door to your nightmares, if you're brave enough."

"I kind of like that game."

"Yes, you seem the type."

Sin laughed, rocking back on his heels. "Thanks." After all, designing computer games, and that one in particular, had made him a lot of money. Money he could now use to design something for pure love, rather than pure profit.

Chastity rose to her feet, awkwardly because the long skirt of her dress was caught under her knee. She tugged on the fabric, stumbled a bit and finally straightened. "Mr. O'Connor. I hate to put a stop to this fascinating discussion, but as you pointed out before, we both have things to do."

Although she was only five foot six or so, from his angle on the floor, Chastity Goodwin suddenly reminded him of a young willow tree, all fluid motion and grace as it swayed with the wind. He remembered an old saying, "Willows bend, but never break." He had no idea why that popped into his mind. He wouldn't have used that image to describe Chastity a few minutes ago. Unyielding oak would have been more to the point. However, the more he watched her, the more his fanciful thought seemed to fit her for some reason. He found that a paradox. Sin's interest sharpened. If there was one thing he lived for, it was to unlock the puzzles that life presented to him.

She bent over him. "Mr. O'Connor? Did you hear me? We only have a few more minutes, remember?"

Sin grinned as he watched her realize she was about to offer him a view of paradise...if paradise was a creamy, female breast. "Hmm."

Flushing as she met his gaze, Chastity abruptly straightened and yanked up the modest scooped bodice of her dress which had slipped to almost reveal a tantalizing curve. *Hic.* She scowled, then flung back her shoulders to take a deep breath. Self-consciously, she attempted to smooth her hair. Not that it did much good, Sin thought. Obviously her mop of copper-colored hair was naturally curly and dampening into wispy kinks because of the summer humidity. Damn but he found her intriguing—hiccups, corkscrew curls, oddities and all.

Rising to his feet, he turned to face her. "Yeah, I heard you, Doc, but...I don't care anymore."

"You what?"

Chastity looked so confused by his comment that he found himself wanting to grab her and hug her. He had no idea when he'd last had so much fun sparring with someone. "I think we should continue our discussion instead."

"Well, I don't."

"I think it's helping your hiccups."

With a sound like an infuriated kitten, Chastity turned and walked over to grab a hanger from the rack, first yanking off a small item and then something larger. She returned and thrust the larger bundle of black in his direction. Chastity pointed toward the self-standing panels by the mirror. "Go behind that screen over there and try these on."

Automatically he took the dark garment. "What's this?"

"It's the bottom of your costume."

He started to unfold the fabric. "My pants?"

"No. Your tights."

"My tights?" He heard his voice hit a note he hadn't hit since the fifth grade when his mother tried to make him sing in the school chorus. "Did you say tights?"

"Yes. Tights." She held out her hand. "Complete with codpiece."

Sin's eyes narrowed as he studied the item dangling from her fingers. It looked like a stuffed sausage, if a sausage could ever be stuffed into velvet, highlighted with metallic trim and then littered with sequins. "What is that?"

"It's the fashion accessory that prevents your getting arrested for indecent exposure when you're wearing your tights."

"Come again?"

"To be historically accurate, the tights have an opening in front where the—*hic*—where your—*hic*—"

Chastity stopped and took a moment to recover her composure. Finally, she tossed her hair back over her shoulders and placed her other hand on her hip in a saucy gesture. Arching her brows, Chastity allowed a wicked laugh to escape. "Well, Sin O'Connor. Perhaps you should think of it as a *padded jockstrap* that you wear on the outside of your clothing."

"A what!" Sin didn't like the look in her eye. Now that she was on familiar ground, he'd lost his advantage. That wasn't acceptable. He lived to push the envelope.

Chastity moved her hand, allowing the codpiece to swing gently. Small flickers of light bounced around the room as the sunlight hit the glittering sequins. "As a matter of *historical* interest, sometimes the codpieces were so fully padded that they became the focus of the entire costume. That's when they became an ornament, instead of a functional item of clothing." Chastity shrugged and her smile sharpened. "Some men needed all the help they could get, you see."

She'd tossed that statement out with a challenging lift to her chin, obviously expecting some response.

Padded? For a moment his customary comebacks deserted him. Sin might be defiant of convention—generally because it was too much trouble to pay attention to it—but in that one moment he realized an eternal masculine truth. Successful as he was, there were still some things a man didn't want to hear. That was one of them.

"Getting back at me for calling you pedantic, Doc?" He lifted his gaze from the clothing ornament swinging in Chastity's hand to take in her slightly mischievous but expectant expression. He focused on the slight lift of her lips. By God, he'd wipe that teasing little smile off her face. "Well, let me make myself perfectly clear, Chastity Goodwin. There is no way you're going to get me into a pair of tights for this wedding."

"You have to wear tights, it's part of the wedding party's—"

He placed his hands on his hips, making sure his fingertips pointed to the item in question as he said, "And my 'anatomy' doesn't need any extra help, thanks very much."

She looked down at the codpiece, the picture of all modesty as she murmured, "I really couldn't say."

"If you're curious, sweetheart, I can supply you with some references." He waited until her stunned gaze lifted to meet his before turning on his heel and walking toward the double doors.

"Mr....uh, Sin. Please, I was only teasing. I don't

know what came over me. Please, I can't have anything go wrong. This is my best friend's wedding!"

"It's *my* brother's." He turned sharply on his heel to face her. "But I'll tell you this. There's no way I'm going to prance around in tights while my brother promises his life away. And there's no way I'm going to let *him* do it, either. Our dad would turn over in his grave."

Chastity hugged the tights close to her chest. "Oh, no, please don't go. Look, I'm sorry I—"

Sin glanced at his watch and said, coolly, "I've decided I have to make that transatlantic call, after all." He knew he was being very rude, but was damned if he'd let this redhead have any more effect on his life than she'd already had. He tried to ignore her face, which was crumpling with distress as she watched him.

Chastity hurried across the room to him. "If it will help, I can try to make some adjustments to the costume so it—"

"The biggest adjustment you can make is to get rid of it."

She froze, clearly affronted by the suggestion. "Or construct it from denim, I suppose?"

Sin indicated his outfit. "That's right—comfortable, well-worn denim."

With a disgusted look on her face, Chastity shook her head. "Why are you so insistent on jeans? Your brother is a veritable fashion plate." She peered at him, making Sin feel like a bug under a microscope. "Are you sure you're related?"

"Not if he's getting married in tights, I'm not."

Chastity hesitated, then a kind—oh, so kind—look settled onto her face. Sin gritted his teeth. It was exactly the kind of look his great-aunt Edna used to give his parents when he'd done something as a teenager that veered toward the scandalous. Not that he deliberately tried to scandalize people. It was just that he was more at home with his computers than he was with people. Sometimes he didn't consider how his actions would affect others. Knowing his weaknesses wasn't going to change his mind, however.

"If you're concerned about how your body will appear in the costume, you needn't be. You have a very nice body. You have no need to feel self-conscious."

"I don't?" Sin spent the time he wasn't creating at the computer either working out or engaging in some type of daredevil physical activity—from motorcycle racing to mountain climbing—so he wasn't sure whether to laugh or question her eyesight.

Chastity patted his arm. "So many men feel like this in the beginning when they see their costume. However, by the time of the wedding they've completely forgotten about it."

"They have, huh?"

"Oh, yes." Chastity stepped a bit closer, anxious to reassure him. "It's part of the fun of the event. You see, no matter what they look like in everyday life, men realize they are actually wonderfully attractive in all of these rich, sumptuous fabrics. It's all part of the pretending."

"The pretending to be part of the past?"

Chastity smiled. "Oh, you'll enjoy it when some saucy maid comes up and flirts with you."

"Are you going to flirt with me?"

"Well…a bit. That's my role at the festival…always teasing but never satisfying."

"Is it, now?" He grinned as he considered her patient expression. You would have thought he was a two-year-old the way she was speaking to him. "Well, perhaps you should show me just how a saucy Renaissance maid flirts with a man, so I know what to be pre-

pared for. That might convince me to consider the costume." He'd teach this wench not to treat him like a
neutered tomcat.

"Well...I'd have a fan that I'd use to good advantage." Chastity thrust the tights into Sin's hands and
pretended to unfurl a fan. Languorously she waved
her hand to and fro before miming the action of hiding
behind the fan as she brought her hand up toward her
face. Suddenly Chastity turned into another woman as
she gave him a flirtatious look before allowing her lids
to lower.

Sin was mesmerized. He stared at Chastity's down-
swept lashes, so long and dark they seemed to throw
shadows onto her cheeks. A small, knowing smile
played around the corner of her lips. Lips which
seemed fuller and riper to Sin than they had before. Sin
could feel his breath come a bit faster as she stepped
closer. He caught a faint hint of an exotic fragrance. Jasmine? Was that only his imagination or was it real? His
blood started to pound as she stood on tiptoe to place
her lips near his ear.

"When the shadows first fall, hasten to the maze, my
lord," she whispered. "There all will be revealed."
Stepping back, she pretended to close her fan. With her
other hand, she kissed her fingers and pressed them
against his lips. Sin was surprised they didn't sizzle
when they touched his mouth.

Damn. She was way too good at this game.

Sin was so confused by Chastity's complete transfor-
mation into a seductress that he tossed his tights aside
and grabbed her wrist to keep her fingers on his lips.
Deliberately he kissed each of her fingertips, ignoring
her gasp and the halfhearted attempt to pull away. His
other arm snaked around her waist and pulled her
close—so close a piece of tissue paper wouldn't have fit
between their bodies. He could feel her heat and her

confusion as she allowed her body to melt against his. He could almost hear her thinking—was he just getting into the spirit of the game? Sin, himself, wasn't sure. He pulled her hand away from his mouth and turned it over to press a kiss into the palm. He chuckled at her gasp. "You're right," he murmured, "this might be fun after all."

"Uh-uh…"

He released her hand and cupped her chin between his thumb and forefinger. He brought her face close to meet his lowering head. He stopped with his lips only centimeters from hers. "And what exactly are you planning to reveal to me in this maze of yours, my lady? How much you want me, perhaps?"

"I don't want you," she practically exhaled the words.

"Oh, no? Well, I want you." Without another word he stopped pretending and let his tongue stroke her ripe mouth. "You taste delicious." He drew back and met her blue eyes. Her pupils were so wide the brilliant blue of her irises was only a halo around her confused desire. And she did desire him. He'd bet on it, even if her hardened nipples pressing against his chest didn't already confirm it. Of course, he hadn't been prepared for how much he'd want her when he first went along with the game.

Not that wanting her was a good idea, or even one he fully understood, he thought. However, that didn't matter. It never did when the fever to press forward and explore the unknown was upon him. Sin lowered his head again to slant his mouth across hers. Eagerly he shaped his lips to hers, allowing his tongue to slip forward to tease. Sin felt her sigh as she flowed into his body. He gathered her closer and settled down to enjoy the ride through space. He'd almost reached the first galaxy when he was interrupted. A man's voice hurled him back to earth with the velocity of an out-of-control rocket.

"Chastity? Daughter, what are you doing?"

The woman in Sin's arms suddenly pushed at his shoulders and leaped away from him. "Father? What are you doing here?"

"I live here, my dear. Remember?"

Sin groaned. Just his luck. A father! More than that, one who was actually called "Father." Immediately he conjured up a vision of a tall, bearded, stern man holding a huge rifle. He glanced at Chastity. No help there. She looked completely mortified.

"I was...we were..."

"You certainly were. And in broad daylight, too."

Sin's ears pricked up. Was that a hint of humor in the man's voice? For the sake of his work and it's unfinished effect on mankind, he sure hoped so.

"Do I know you, young man?"

Sin sent Chastity a quizzical look, but she avoided his eyes. There was no hope for it. Time to face the music. Hell. He'd never been any good at this. That's why his dating life was strictly limited to the types of women who didn't have a stone-faced guardian lurking in the vicinity. Unable to avoid it, Sin squared his shoulders and turned around, automatically looking up to face the towering presence of the man behind him.

There was no one there.

Sin looked down. There standing in front of him was a small man with white hair and skin that was tanned to the shade of light-brown leather. Deep wrinkles fanned out from his bright blue eyes. Eyes his daughter had obviously inherited. The man's eyes gleamed as they met Sin's. Were they twinkling? Or was that a trick of the light?

"Hmm, seems not. I can only hope my daughter does."

Sin was stunned speechless; first by not seeing the huge monstrous dad he'd expected to see, and secondly by the crisp snowy-white, minister's collar that clasped under the man's droopy chin. The older man laced his fingers together over the round-as-a-robin abdomen that swelled the front of the black clerical waistcoat.

Chastity rushed into speech. "Father, this is Harrison O'Connor's brother. I was measuring him for his best man's—"

"You were measuring him?"

"*Hic.*" Chastity's skin turned to flame and her sprinkling of freckles stood out like measles. "Well, not then, *hic*, before though…before I was."

Yep, Chastity's father's eyes were definitely twinkling, but Sin doubted his daughter realized it. Chastity was too busy babbling and hiccuping as she tried to salvage the situation. Sin's embarrassment receded as his sense of the ridiculous leaped forward to take its place.

"New technique, Reverend Goodwin," he explained with a laconic shrug.

"So I gather."

"Father—*hic*—I can explain."

Sin turned to Chastity. "Can you? 'Cause I can't."

She was so taken aback and adorably embarrassed that Sin was tempted to kiss her again for the sheer pleasure of having her try to explain the action.

Chastity blinked. "What do you mean?"

"One minute we were talking about tights and the next we were—"

"That only happened because you refused to consider wearing—"

"I still refuse."

Chastity flung her arms wide and turned to her father. "Father, tell him he has to wear tights to this wedding. He's the best man for heaven's sake! How will it look if he shows up in jeans?"

Sin folded his arms. "I'll look like the only sensible man in the place."

Reverend Goodwin hid his chuckle behind a slight cough. "Ah, this man—" he looked quizzically toward Sin, who was quick to sense his cue.

"Sin O'Connor."

"Sin?" For the first time, the reverend seemed discomfited. His gaze darted from Sin to his daughter before dancing back to Sin to size him up. After a moment he looked pleased, as if he were smiling inside. "Chastity," he lingered over the word, peeking again at both of them before stroking his chin. "Where was I? Ah, yes...as I was saying, this man has a point."

"No, he doesn't. He's being selfish and rude. He's putting himself before his brother. More important, he's putting himself before the bride's feelings. Brigit has her heart set on this wedding being as authentic as possible."

Reverend Goodwin arched a brow in Sin's direction. "It seems my daughter also has a point."

Rarely had Sin been slapped down so gently, and so thoroughly. But the devil in him wouldn't let him completely admit it. "I'll speak with my brother about it."

Before Chastity could continue the attack, her father moved in for the kill. "Good idea. I'm sure you'll come to the right decision."

Feeling like a small boy who'd had been caught raiding the cookie jar, Sin looked for a way out. He found it on his wrist. "Look at the time. I have to call Japan."

Chastity stepped toward him, obviously not wanting to be alone with her father. "I'll see you to the door."

Sin was having none of that. "Don't trouble yourself. I know the way. Good to have met both of you."

After stooping to pick up the tights from the floor, Chastity moved forward, saying, "It's no troub—"

"No, no. Not necessary." Sin backed toward the door. He was leaving this house under his own steam. Without any escort who would confuse him about the afternoon's happenings any further.

Hearing Chastity's footsteps behind him and feeling as if a thousand furies were after him, he strode through the front room, then turned into the hallway and headed straight out the door. At the moment Sin felt as if he were trapped in his own computer game. Except he was no longer the all-knowing scientist, but the unlucky visitor floundering around in a series of nightmares.

With any luck, he'd stumble across the path to sweet dreams.

CHASTITY STEPPED into the hallway, watching as Sin O'Connor strode toward the front door. By the effect he'd had on her during the past hour, she expected to see him disappear in a flash of fire, leaving behind the smell of brimstone. She couldn't understand how one man could cause such chaos.

She reached the door just as Sin slammed through it. No. Her life was far from chaotic. Even in the midst of a childhood most would describe as unique as she'd traveled from one anthropology site to another with her parents there'd been an order and a certainty to her existence. So much so that she never questioned her world, her place in it or her destiny, which was quite unlike many of the individuals in the Renaissance era she so admired. A flash of insight made her wonder if that was one of the reasons she had adopted that particular period as her own. Chastity bit her lip. She'd never questioned her love for history until Sin disrupted her life with his insinuations about the security available in her familiar academic world.

Opening the door a crack she watched him gun his bike and roar up the street. "Damn you," she whispered. "I don't care what you think. I'm not living in some safe little bubble."

3

CLOSING THE DOOR, Chastity slowly walked back to the study to face her father.

He stood by the window, obviously having watched as Sin sped away. "Hmm, interesting young man, Chastity."

"He's a menace," she muttered darkly.

Her father laughed. "Hardly that, my dear. Although I can see he has quite an effect on you."

Chastity could feel the blood rushing to her cheeks at her father's observation. Still unable to face him without turning even redder, she murmured over her shoulder, "It's probably the full moon or something."

"Yes, that would be the reason you were kissing him in the middle of the afternoon," her father agreed dryly.

Chastity turned to face him then. "Well, I don't have any other explanation."

"You don't?" He chuckled. "Chastity, I think you've spent far too much time in a classroom."

"Don't be silly, Father...as if anyone ever could." Chastity felt like a research specimen under her parent's piercing stare. She hunched her shoulders and looked down at the worn wood floor, trying to protect her thoughts from his sharp assessment. After all, this was the man who'd helped people see into their souls at her mother's research sites. If he really decided to look into hers, Chastity didn't stand a chance.

"Oh, my dear little girl." She felt his hand drop onto

her shoulder and give a gentle squeeze. "I would hate to think my moving in here with you while your mother is in South America is...cramping your style, shall I say?"

At that, Chastity turned and looked him almost square in the eye. "Of course it isn't. I don't have that much style to cramp." She smiled into his twinkling blue eyes. "I asked you to come because I couldn't see you ratttling around in that big old house for a year without Mother."

He gave her a wistful smile in return. "It does get rather lonely without her. She's never been gone this long. She's such a vibrant presence."

"Father. Did you ever wish Mother was more typical? I mean, she's always traipsing around the world studying societies that are *uncomfortable* at best. Sometimes, don't you wish she'd chuck it all and stay safe with you?"

"She wouldn't be your mother if she did that." He patted her hand. "I know it was hard on you sometimes, honey."

Chastity sighed. "Not when we were gone, but it wasn't easy to fit in with the other kids when we came back home. Not too many thirteen-year-old girls can give a discourse about the prepuberty rituals of the Waraganda tribe without appearing rather odd."

"I know, honey. Children can be little beasts."

Grimacing, Chastity agreed, "And how."

"Still, I believe people have to be what they are—inside, I mean. People can grow and develop, but what's inside from the very beginning always tells true. Perhaps it's destiny." He grinned with pride. "Take your mother. Inside she's a pure adventurer, so you can't hold her back. She's also a whiz of a researcher and scholar, but anthropology isn't a tidy textbook subject."

Chastity sighed. "With her accomplishments, Mother's hard to live up to."

"You shouldn't try, my dear. You'll have enough of a time living up to your own potential, much less trying to wear someone else's clothes. Realizing where you really belong is half the challenge, you know." Her father put his arm around Chastity's shoulders. "Take me, for example. I decided I needed a church, a permanent one, not just a temporary ministry. That meant I had to stay put, not travel around with your mother. But we decided that wouldn't affect the way she ran her career."

"I guess twenty years of doing that was enough for you, huh?"

"Twenty years, plus the challenge of trying to provide some type of normal life for our child during it all—" he chuckled and squeezed her "—was about as much adventure as I needed. But I underestimated myself. Now I go into the unknown every time I counsel a person in trouble, or help an individual come to terms with the limits of their reality. I find that thrilling, actually."

Chastity looked at her father. He'd sent chills down her spine with that statement. "How odd. I've never thoguht of what you did that way."

Smiling, he let her go. "It took me quite a while to discover it myself."

Does one ever know someone else? Chastity wondered. She thought she'd always known who her father was. Now she was confused to discover he was so much more than she'd imagined.

Sin O'Connor's face popped into her mind, complete with all of his devil-may-care charm and the challenging glint in his eyes. It wasn't difficult to imagine making new discoveries about him. However, when she tried to picture herself finding new realizations about

Jeremy George many years from now it was difficult. Chastity shook her head. That was only because she'd known Jeremy longer, not because Sin was more...*anything*.

Her old cuckoo clock announced the half hour. "My, my, three-thirty already," her father confirmed as he removed his pocket watch to double-check.

"Oh, no. I...Father, I have to go and change. I'm meeting Jeremy for tea at the castle."

Her father chuckled. "Be careful you don't run into Sin O'Connor again."

"I doubt he's staying there. The new motel in town is more his speed. A man like Sin O'Connor doesn't have Jeremy's reverence for antiquity and order and... tradition."

"Not many people do," Reverend Goodwin said in a dry-as-ancient-dust tone.

Chastity glanced at her father, suddenly feeling like a little girl seeking reasssurance. "You like Jeremy, don't you?" Why was she doubting her own judgment all of a sudden? She hadn't made any decisions about a future with Jeremy, regardless of how much he assumed.

"Well, or course I do, my dear. He's a very pleasant man." Reverend Goodwin agreed.

Chastity frowned. She'd always taken it for granted that her father felt the man in question was perfect for his daughter. Now she wondered. Was there a hint of reserve in her father's voice, after all? Surely she was imagining things. Obviously today's episode with Sin had taken a toll on her.

"Sin is such an interesting name, don't you think, Chastity?"

Sin—such an exotic presence in the small, everyday world she now made her life. Chastity swallowed the urge to hiccup. She was still mortified at her physical response to a perfect stranger. An image of his face slipped into her thoughts again, this time sharp and tense with desire. She could still feel the pressure of his lips, the stroke of his tongue. Chastity shivered.

"Cold?"

"No. Hot," Chastity blurted. "That is..." She couldn't say another word. She could only pray her face wasn't as red as a ripe, Italian tomato. Damn Sin O'Connor. It was all his fault she looked like an absolute idiot in front of her father! She tried to imagine all sorts of bloodthirsty tortures to punish him. Sin stretched full-length on the rack, chained to a wall, stripped to the waist— *Oh, my!*

"I like his motorcycle," her father dropped his observaiton into the silence.

Brought back to earth, Chastity searched wildly for a frame of reference. Jeremy. They'd been talking about Jeremy. "Jeremy has a motorcycle? I didn't know that."

"Not Jeremy. Sin."

"Oh. Him." She thought of her first sight of Sin as he'd dismounted and stalked toward the door. He'd made the day seem only marginally hotter than he had been. The temperature of her thoughts was still near boiling range, thanks to him.

Reverend Goodwin nodded thoughtfully, "That type of bike suits Sin O'Connor, right down to the ground."

"And under it," she muttered. Chastity folded her arms, hugging Sin's discarded tights close. Just hearing his name on her father's lips made her realize how totally unsuitable the man was. *Sin*. She stared at her father for a moment before replying, "Yes, it does, Father. That motorcycle is totally irresponsible, noisy and annoying. Just like he is."

SIN'S EARS were burning. If he'd been superstitious, he would have thought someone was talking about him. But he knew better. He knew it was because he'd forgotten to put on his helmet when he'd started his cycle. He'd been too concerned with putting as much distance between him and Chastity Goodwin as possible. His ears were burning from the dry, heated wind that was whipping past him as he roared out of town.

He turned left off the main street and hit the open country road outside the small, charming gingerbread town where Chastity lived. He shifted gears and really opened it up. Then engine responded with an accelerated whine and the heavily wooded countryside was a blur as he sped past.

Chastity Goodwin. Give him strength. He might as well have locked lips with a vestal virgin as this woman. Except she sure didn't behave like an untouchable maiden. One touch and he'd almost burned up.

Chastity Goodwin.

With a name like that, wouldn't you know she'd have a minister for a father! Although, Sin had to admit, for a minister, Chastity's dad seemed like a pretty cool character. He'd like to get to know him better, but definitely under different circumstances.

He hadn't meant to kiss her. The idea sort of took hold of him and before he knew it he was sinking into her innate passion and her father was interrupting. It was pretty funny now that he thought about it. Sin wondered what his brother would think? He could hear him now—

You did what? Honestly, Sin, have you nothing better to do with your time than hunt down the most untouchable woman in the county and put the make on her?

Untouchable.

Sin hadn't found her so. But it was a bit strange for a

woman in her late twenties to live with her father, wasn't it? What did that say about her? That she was shy, repressed, afraid to face the world without an authority figure by her side? Sin squinted as he scanned the road up ahead. He hadn't found her any of those things, either. Instead he'd found her energetic, opinionated and sexy as hell! As a matter of fact, she was such a contradiction he now had a headache.

He wished he could blame *that* on forgetting his helmet, but truth was he'd been disoriented from the minute he'd walked to the door and run into the woman. She'd reminded him of the delicate illustrations of King Arthur's wife, Guinevere. Unfortunately, he'd never been too fond of history. He much preferred looking forward than back. Maybe Chastity had cast a spell over him, like Sin's evil scientist did when the unwary entered his game world.

"Yeah, right...get real."

Still, he had problems understanding his reaction to her. No one was further from being the type of woman who usually attracted him than Chastity Goodwin. It didn't matter. His libido had revved up and slammed into overdrive the minute he'd held that redheaded, storybook heroine in his arms.

Harrison was going to laugh his buns off when he found out about this.

Thinking of his brother brought his attention back to the road and the fact that he'd better start looking for the turnoff to Ravenswood. He almost missed the small sign peeking from the shrubbery by the side of the road and turned so sharply onto the gravel driveway that he almost upset his bike. *Idiot*, he told himself. *Pay attention. Now's not the time to kill yourself.*

He slowed down as he followed the winding road through the woods, climbing toward the summit. The trees were fully canopied at this time of year, creating a dark, mysterious feeling that reached deep inside him. It made him think of winding corridors and forbidden delights. A new game idea, perhaps? Or maybe it was symbolic of the beginning of a relationship. *Now where the hell had that idea come from?* He could see a fanciful Renaissance lover like Chastity having that kind of re-action, but not a cool, possessed visionary of the future like himself.

The shadowed lane immediately opened up to re-veal a scene from a fairy tale…or a fantasy computer game. Sin slowed his bike to a stop, and flung out his legs to dig his heels into the ground to keep his bal-ance. There in front of him, in all its historical glory, was a castle…a three-story pile of creamy stone and turrets, mullioned windows and heavy wooden doors. His gaze was drawn to the flags depicting dragons and mystical beasts that marked the curving towers. All that was missing was Chastity Goodwin, waving her kerchief to welcome him home from his travels.

"Oh, that's it," he muttered, rubbing his eyes. "I've got to get more sleep."

Slipping his cycle into gear, he lifted his heels and approached the front of the castle where the entrance beckoned. He parked in between a racy sports car, that no doubt belonged to his brother, and a serviceable sports utility vehicle. After unbuckling his duffel bag from the back of the cycle he hefted it over his shoulder and strolled toward what would be his home for the next six days.

A sea of blue flowers swayed gently in the breeze in a rippling display that reminded him of water being lightly kissed by the wind. Sin pulled off his sun-glasses, tucking them into the top of his T-shirt, won-dering if this flower "moat" was a touch of humor from his relative-to-be. He sure hoped so. A week spent with a complete history purist was a week too

much, in his opinion. Unless it was a week with the
Doc.

"Ah, hell, now where did that come from?"

"Still talking to yourself, Sin? You really need a life!"

Startled, Sin pulled his gaze from the dancing blue
blossoms and looked toward the door. There, up under
the covered portico, one of the massive wooden doors
had quietly opened to reveal his brother. For a second,
Sin took stock of him. His brother still had the devas-
tating good looks that he'd possessed as the star quar-
terback of Millwood High, but after years of travel and
being in a powerful position, he was smooth and polished. And women loved it. Sin wondered about his
soon-to-be sister-in-law. Harrison's taste had always
run to sophisticated society beauties with perfect
taste—not an enthusiastic bimbo among them.

"Hey, there. You look about the same."

Harrison grinned. "Think so?"

"Well, maybe." Sin cocked his head, narrowing his
eyes at the tall, slender man in the doorway. Now that
Sin took a really hard look, there was a subtle difference. Maybe it was the way Harrison held himself, or
the look on his face. Or?

"Wait a minute. It's your hair. Damn, Harrison, I've
never seen it that long. It's as long as mine—almost
down to your collar. Not quite *GQ* material anymore,
are you?"

Harrison gave a self-conscious shrug that lifted the
shoulders of his perfectly fitting knit Polo shirt. "It's
for the wedding. More in the period, you see."

Groaning, Sin walked forward to join his brother under the stone arched porch. "Oh, no. Not you, too."

"Well, if you want to look the part—'

Holding up his hand like a school crossing guard,
Sin cut him off. "I just had one person lecturing me

about period correctness. I don't need to hear it from my own brother."

Laughing, Harrison punched Sin's shoulder. "Still as charming as ever."

Sin ignored his brother. Instead his attention was caught by the suit of armor standing guard by the door. "Is this guy gonna let me in, or do I have to tip him?"

Harrison laughed. "You'd be surprised what people put in there. Brigit says she's cleaned out gum wrappers, cigar butts, you name it. Of course the strangest was the condom."

Sin's curiosity was piqued. "Still in the package, I hope?"

Shrugging, Harrison reached for Sin's bag. "I could never get her to tell me." He stepped toward the door, looking over his shoulder to say curiously, "Who was lecturing you?"

"Well, since I had to stop by to see my best man duds, I'll give ya one guess."

"It had to be Chastity. She and Brigit get together and start talking about the 'old days' as if they'd been living under a leaf in the forest during the entire sixteenth century."

Sin shivered. "Brigit is really into history, too?" Then he shook his head as he walked into the three-story great hall just inside the castle entrance. "Stupid question, I guess. Why else would she do all this?"

Harrison stopped inside the archway. "Well, Brigit does love history, but she also loves to make a dollar." Harrison indicated the castle. "After all, this kind of B-and-B setting in the middle of America's nowhere is unique. And unique sells."

Sin rubbed his chin. "I gotta tell you. I can't picture you content to stay put in the middle of nowhere. What happened to that internationally focused big-time career?"

"At the moment, I'm tired of it." Harrison shrugged. "Who knows what I'll do later. I've got some ideas. Maybe we'll take this castle concept and start a chain."

Putting aside his initial prejudice, Sin took stock of the room. His gaze first fell on the magnificent floor-to-ceiling stone fireplace, then continued to travel around the room, taking in the rich paneling that rose to the top of the wall before hitting a creamy stucco-and-raftered ceiling. The middle of one long wall at the back of the room was pierced by French doors leading to a deck that looked out over the serene hillsides and forests. Sin whistled. "You could be right about this place, Harry." To the right, dominating the entire wall, were three huge stained-glass windows. The yellows, oranges, reds and dark blues of the windows glowed so brightly in the afternoon light, Sin could almost imagine Father Sun had painted itself with brilliant tattoos to pay a visit to Mother Earth. He made a mental note to use that image in his next game.

Harrison indicated the doorways and other stairways that led off the great room at each corner. "Those lead to bedrooms and suites on all floors."

"Where did you put me?"

"Upstairs. Third floor."

The lack of expression on Harrison's face as he answered warned Sin to go cautiously. "What's the catch?"

"No catch. Follow me." Harrison walked behind and around Sin then started up the stairs to the right.

Sprinting after him, Sin closed the distance to follow behind. He thunked Harrison in the back with his fist. "When we were kids I learned never to trust you when you spoke in that careful tone." Sin pushed him a bit harder, causing his brother to stumble into the second floor hallway. "Now give."

Harrison chuckled. "Nope. It's a surprise." Using that comment as the perfect red-flag-to-a-bull statement, Harrison started to sprint down the hallway and head toward a narrow set of stairs at the back. Sin was close behind. Together they thundered up the steps. As usual, Sin choose the expedient approach and used his forward momentum and position to launch himself from the last step.

"Damn it, Sin," Harrison yelled.

"You're dead meat." Sin hit him low and grabbed his brother around the knees in a perfect football tackle. *Why couldn't I ever do that on a football field?* He'd been terrible at football...but dynamite on the squash court.

Harrison tried to dislodge Sin as they fell through the bedroom door at the top of the stairs. "Get off me, you maniac."

"No way." They crashed onto the floor and rolled, once then twice. Finally Sin got the upper hand and levered himself onto his older-by-ten-months-and-don't-you-forget-it brother, managing, just barely, to pin him to the ground. That's when he realized he was looking at rose-pink carpet and was so surprised that he momentarily lost control of the situation.

That was all the opening Harrison needed to buck Sin off and grab him in a headlock. "You never were any good at this, computer boy," Harrison grunted.

Sin ignored him. Unfortunately, he'd just caught sight of the delicate rosebuds that decorated the wall, and the trailing lace that kissed the windows. It sent all other thoughts from his mind. He didn't even protest when his brother twisted his neck a bit more and rubbed a big, bruising knuckle-noogie onto his scalp with his fist.

"Sin, what the hell is wrong with you? You used to hate it when I rubbed your head like that."

Sin finally reacted to the alarm in his brother's voice. "I still hate it."

Harrison let him go and sat back on his heels. "Did I hurt you or something?"

"You couldn't hurt me if you had all week." Old childhood habits died hard, Sin thought. No matter how much time had passed it wasn't long before they were acting like ten-year-olds. Their relationship had always been that way. "But this room…this room is another story."

"What are you talking about?"

Stunned, Sin sat up and with a painful expression pointed to the elaborate, canopy bed that dominated the room. To the appreciative—his new sister-in-law, perhaps—it was a delicate bower that presented a field of dainty flowers, with the bed covering consisting of draped laces and floating net dripping with leaves and delicate flowers. To Sin, it was a fussy, misguided elaboration.

"Wh-wh—" He lost his ability to say a word as he continued to gaze around the room. As if the bed and the colors weren't enough, there, just above the bed was a heart-shaped window to invite the nighttime stars inside. It was too much for a man who spent half his night walking around, thinking and working instead of sleeping.

"What the hell is this? I keep expecting to see Robin Whatsis-name come swinging through here on a vine."

Laughing, Harrison replied, "That's Tarzan who does that, you ape. Not Robin Hood."

Sin waved his hand. "Whatever. There's no way I'm staying in this historical powder puff of a room for a night, much less six days."

"You have to. Rapunzel's Bower was the only room left, that's why Brigit gave it to you."

"What did you call it?"

"All the rooms have names. Knight's Passion, M'Lady's Kiss, Rapunzel's Bower. It's kind of cute, really."

"Cute? Oh, my God, you must be in love. Only a total lunatic could find anything remotely appealing in cute little names and sweet little decorations and…" He leaned back onto his elbows and stared at his brother. *Yep, he looked different, all right.*

Harrison's blond hair, as light as his own was dark, seemed to shine with a new radiance, his golden-brown eyes, the only feature remotely resembling Sin's coloring, were glowing with good humor, his finely chiseled cheekbones and sculpted jaw looked softer than usual. All in all, this was a much more approachable man than Sin could ever remember. He almost didn't recognize him, after all.

"What in the holy hell is with you?" He hadn't seen this coming. It had all happened in fast forward, but still—how could he have lost touch with his brother so completely?

Harrison rubbed his finger over his nose in an almost shy gesture. "You're right. I'm head over heels in love, Sin. I don't know how it happened, and I don't remember when it did exactly. I mean, I was walking along a street in Paris, and there she was…standing there looking kind of lost. That was it."

"No, come on. My smooth-as-a-backstroke brother fell in love at first sight?" Sin felt a bit of a tingle at that, but he wasn't sure why. Obviously, it didn't really happen. Harrison just thought it did.

Scratching his head, seeming as confused as Sin, Harrison agreed, "I guess so. All I know is, I wouldn't change one minute of what's happening in my life now for all the minutes on earth."

Sin sighed. "One more good man bites the dust."

Harrison punched his brother on the arm. "Wait 'til you meet Brigit. You'll love her."

"I hope not. I've got enough problems with the woman I just met." For some reason thinking of Brigit, the tall smooth blonde to come, reminded him of another tall, smo— Sin stopped there. Smooth? Nope, not on a bet. Kind of gawky, actually—redhead.

"Who was...oh, Chastity?"

Shuddering, Sin nodded. "Yeah...she packs a punch like a tire jack."

"You're talking about Chastity Goodwin?"

"Uh-huh."

Harrison arched his eyebrow and tilted his head. "What did you do that she had to punch you?"

"Nothing. Not that kind of punch." Sin looked away, unable to meet Harrison's probing gaze. "I only meant the damn woman got to me without my knowing how she—" He scowled and turned away. "Never mind. I think it was my imagination. That and I probably need something to eat. I'm starving."

Harrison bent over to pick up Sin's duffel, hefting it onto the luggage stand. "The tearoom's open. Brigit does a real English tea in the afternoons. It's been a big seller. People are coming from miles around."

"Brigit really does have a mercenary streak."

"She's one hell of a businesswoman."

"Well, I can deal with that, I guess." Sin looked around the dainty pink-green-and-white room. "It's some of the other aspects of her personality I'll have a bit more of a problem with."

Harrison clasped his brother's shoulder. "You'll get used to it. Hell, your eyes will be closed when you're up here anyway."

"Not with my sleeping habits, they won't."

"Oh, yeah, I forgot you're a night owl." Harrison grinned and led the way to the door. "Maybe you can find a good book downstairs in the library—or a good woman, somewhere."

"Just because you're getting married doesn't mean I want to."

"Who knows—" Harrison ignored his brother and continued "—you might even find this place grows on you."

Sin shuddered as he looked over his shoulder at the dreamy lace caressing the bed. Then he cast a gloomy eye in his brother's direction as he reached the hallway. "I guess you're really going to wear tights to the wedding, aren't you?"

Harrison turned. "Well, of course. It's part of the ambiance of the Renaissance event. Besides, Brigit wants me to. It's very important to her that this be historically correct."

The ambiance of the event. Lord, help me. From the signs his besotted brother had been giving him, Sin should have been prepared to have his worst nightmares confirmed. However, he'd hoped to change Harrison's mind. Now he could see it wouldn't be worth the effort. "I want to go on record that this is taking brotherly love way too far. You'll owe me."

"No problem." Harrison stepped eagerly to the stairs, saying over his shoulder, "Come on, Sin, let's track Brigit down and get something to tide you over until dinner."

Sin took a last look at his room and sighed. Shaking his head, he turned to follow his brother's eager clatter down the steps. For the sake of Harrison and his Brigit, he'd have to give in to the inevitable—even if the inevitable was tights and a codpiece. But Sin was determined not to confess that to Chastity Goodwin until he was good and ready.

I'll let her stew for a while. End of the week should do it. By that time, he'd be better prepared to face her anyway. After all, he was positive he'd exaggerated her impact on him. From this point on, he was immune to all redheads named Chastity. And he'd stay that way.

He couldn't wait to prove it.

Sin followed his brother through the great room and along a winding corridor to a small door that led outside. Harrison was moving so rapidly it was as if he'd been away from his fiancée for a week. "I appreciate the way you're thinking of my stomach," Sin said, "but slow down. I'm getting a stitch in my side."

Harrison paused, one hand on the doorknob. "Sorry. I was thinking about Brigit."

"When did you see her last?"

"An hour ago, after we got back from the grocery store." His brother gave a goofy smile that reminded Sin of the time they'd gotten a puppy for Christmas.

Whistling softly, Sin said, "This Brigit of yours must really be something."

Harrison flushed to the roots of his blond hair. "I can't explain it. When I'm not with her, I'm thinking about her. When I am with her, I don't want to leave her. I can't get away from it."

"It sounds like a disease. One I don't want to catch."

Laughing, Harrison grabbed his brother's arm and yanked him through the door into the courtyard. "You'll get yours, pal. Wait and see if you don't."

"No way do I want a woman invading me like a virus. I've got too much to do to get involved with something that time consuming."

Lifting a brow, Harrison replied, "Yeah. That's what I said. Right before I went under for the third time." He walked down the stone path to a large round stone tower, whose discrete sign proclaimed, Ye Old Tearoom. Harrison stopped by a picturesque wooden door. "Let's see about filling that stomach of yours before the place gets too crowded. Brigit makes great cucumber sandwiches."

"Are you nuts? Two seconds and I'll be starving again. Love might have made you lose your appetite, but mine's just fine."

Harrison grinned. "It's so easy to wind you up, Sin. Okay, no cucumber. Brigit makes these mouthwatering meat pies and pastries that—" His words were abruptly cut off when a small woman with brown hair cut into a pixie style bustled through the door and barreled into him.

"I'm sorry I didn't— Oh, hi, honey." The woman changed the apology into a bear hug which, from her lack of inches, resembled a bear cub hugging a towering oak tree.

Sin watched in amazement as his brother hugged her back, then lifted her up to plant a deep kiss on her mouth. *This* was Brigit? Where was the tall, sleek blond beauty he'd expected? The woman in his brother's arms reminded him of an unmade bed, all rumply and comfortable. Definitely not Harrison's type.

Harrison set Brigit back onto her feet. "Darling, you have to quit leaping through the doorways. You'll run down one of our customers." He tucked Brigit into the crook of his arm and turned. "Sin. This is Brigit."

Sin took his time, looking her over very thoroughly. For his brother's sake, he tried to keep his thoughts hidden, but it was difficult. Dressed in leggings and some type of white overshirt, the woman reminded him of an elf. Brigit was petite—five foot two was stretching it—with a little triangle of a face, shell-like ears and large brown eyes that sparkled at him the longer he stared.

"Not what you were expecting, huh?"

Sin could feel a blush rising from the collar of his T-shirt. "Well..." He glanced at his brother. Sin didn't want to hurt his feelings by commenting, but she'd left him no choice. "You're different from the—"

"Ice-cold, frosty-blond beauty-queen types your brother used to date?" Chuckling, Brigit reached up and patted Harrison's cheek before her attention returned to Sin. "Funny, he said the same thing."

Getting in the spirit, Sin said, "Was that before or after he proposed?"

"Oh, before...and after." Brigit grinned and walked toward Sin, holding out her left hand. "Tell you the truth, I think this whole wedding thing is still a bit of a shock to him."

Sin took Brigit's hand in both of his and looked down at the huge diamond sparking in the sunlight. "I don't blame him a bit. My brother's announcement took me by surprise, too."

Harrison leaned back against the door. "Wait until it happens to you. When you meet the right woman and fall in love, Sinclair O'Connor, I'll laugh all the way down the aisle."

"No, you won't. 'Cause I'm going to see it coming and run the other way."

"Harrison told me you were a confirmed bachelor." Brigit gave Harrison a sly little look. "But then, so was he."

Sin dropped her hand and jumped back like a man who'd just stepped on a snake. "Since you're going to be my sister, I might as well speak plainly. Get that matchmaking look out of your eye."

"My brother has a point, darling. You were asking about fixing him up with one of your friends."

"That was before I met him. Now I don't think Julie would do for him."

Alarmed, Sin automatically went into denial mode. "Wait a minute. I'm perfectly happy with my single status. I have no intention of losing it."

Brigit gave him such an irrepressible chuckle that Sin couldn't help grinning in response. "Definitely not Julie. I'll have to think of someone else."

"Sin met Chastity Goodwin this afternoon, darling."

As Harrison dropped that little tidbit into the conversation, Sin regretted not annihilating his brother earlier—in their childhood, before he'd had the chance to develop into a full-grown snake. Sin *really* regretted it as a thoughtful expression settled onto Brigit's face.

"Chastity?" Brigit let her gaze wander casually over him, reminding him of a skinny cat inspecting a plump mouse. "Tempting, but Chastity's practically off-limits."

"What?" Sin could feel the hairs on the back of his neck standing up in reaction to Brigit's sharp little announcement. "Off-limits how? Engaged?"

"Not that, but she's been seeing someone on a regular basis for the past few years." Brigit cocked her head with birdlike curiosity. "Why?"

"No reason." It was best for all concerned if he dropped the subject right now. Sin didn't even know why he was pursuing it. What did he care if Chastity Goodwin was involved? The woman meant nothing to him. If she appeared right in front of him, right now, he'd look at her and feel nothing. That kiss had been a spur-of-the-moment thing. Meaningless.

"Oh, well, I'll come up with something." Brigit shrugged philosophically then turned to her fiancé. "Could you help Allison watch the tearoom for a bit, honey? I have to get some information from my office for old Mrs. Mertson and I have some phone calls to return. The tearoom's not too busy and most of our castle guests haven't even arrived yet." After a quick kiss and a "Back soon," Brigit was gone in a blur before Harrison could agree.

Grinning, Harrison said, "Let's go inside and get you something to eat. If you get any paler you might pass out."

"Why is it when a woman's getting married, she's not happy unless everyone else in the world is getting married, too?"

Harrison opened the door and motioned his brother inside. "Beats me. Maybe it's in their hormones, or their genes."

Sin stepped into the room, saying as he passed his brother, "Personally, I'm better off when my hormones stay in my jeans. That way I won't get into any trouble."

Harrison laughed. "Hold that thought, brother. It might get you back home alive—and single."

Chuckling, Sin headed for a table by the tall counter. Pulling out a chair he stepped over it, mounting it like the black beast he'd ridden in on. He grinned as Harry slid elegantly into a chair opposite him like the sophisticate he was. At least some things never changed. As Harry was crooking his finger for the waitress, Sin studied the menu. With a wink for the plump young woman who'd bustled over, he ordered a number four and five with a long, tall tank of cider before finally fixing his gaze back on his brother.

"Alive and single, huh? Trust me, Harry, the woman hasn't been born yet who can put a collar and a bell on me."

4

SIN WAS JUST BITING into the most delicious hunk of meat pie he'd ever eaten when the door opened. Looking across the sparsely populated tea room he saw Chastity Goodwin enter, accompanied by a dignified-looking man in his late thirties. The man was wearing studious horn-rimmed glasses and a lightweight tweed sport soat. She paused in the doorway while the man leaned down to whisper in her ear, his proprietary hand clasping her arm.

Sin gulped, attempting to swallow the bite of beef before he choked. He ran his tongue around his lips to lap up a stray bit of gravy as he stared at the woman across the room. Chastity looked as delicious as the fragrant pastry in his hands. He could practically feel a collar around his neck when his eyes connected with hers. So much for being completely unaffected by her presence. His hormones started to riot as his gaze skimmed from her curly topknot of hair past her wide blue eyes, to her yummy lips pursed and slightly opened in shock, then down the long white neck rising swanlike from her rounded collar. His mouth watered as he got a sudden image of stroking his tongue down her graceful neck until he reached the full breasts rounding the bodice of her prim, flowered dress. Sin could almost see her hard nipples jutting against the material as they begged for his touch. Strangely, the ladylike restraint of her clothing was enough to drive a man nuts. With that type of challenge, what red-blooded male could help but respond? Sin's perusal shifted to the guy next to her. The thought of him having the same thoughts maddened him. His hand clenched to a fist. Flakes of pastry flecked the lace tablecloth.

"Sin?"

Ignoring his brother, Sin snapped his gaze back to Chastity. The impulse to pull her into his arms and seek her lips was so strong that he pushed back his chair, starting to rise. All he could think of was tasting those pursed lips again. One taste wasn't enough. He wanted to plunge his tongue into her sweetness, savor her, devour her...make her beg.

"Sin." Harry's voice got through. "What're you doing?"

Sin jerked his gaze down to see his brother staring up at him. "Huh?"

"Are you going to eat that pie or just squeeze the hell out of it?"

Looking down, Sin unclenched his fist to take a good look at the mangled mess he'd made of his lunch. He dropped it back on the plate and picked up his napkin. "I was—" He hadn't the vaguest idea what he was doing. Luckily his brother removed his curious glance to peer over his shoulder at the two new customers at the door.

Harry snapped Sin a look. "Ah...I see."

"What do you see?" Sin scowled and settled back with a thump. "Never mind."

Harry chuckled as he stood up. He muttered from the side of his mouth, "Alive or single. Which will it be?"

His scowl deepened. "Leave it alone, Harry."

Brows almost risen to full mast, Harry said, "Are you kidding? Would you leave it alone?"

"That's different. You're nicer than I am."

Harry's grin assumed wolfish proportions. "Only on the surface."

"Right." Sin tilted his head to consider his ever suave elder brother. "I've forgotten how ruthless a businessman you can be."

"Don't give me that innocent look. It runs in the family."

Sin's gaze speared Chastity as she remained frozen inside the doorway. "Only when I see something I want."

With a small chuckle, Harry followed his gaze and said, "Anything come to mind?"

"Maybe." Hastily he added, "Temporarily at least." He wasn't looking for an involvement. He had too much to do…too much to accomplish.

"Chastity doesn't appear to be a temporary type of woman."

Now Sin smiled, feeling a lot more sure of himself as he watched Chastity react to his stare. The flush bloomed first on her cheeks then the tip of her nose. "Anyone is that type of woman if the temptation is right."

Harry shook his head and turned to face the door. He waved the couple over to their table, muttering under his breath.

"What'd you say, Har?"

"I said, the temptation being you?"

Sin nodded at his brother without taking his eyes off Chastity. "It works both ways. Tempter…temptee."

Harry leaned down to whisper in Sin's ear. "Watch yourself. I think you've got the wrong playmate here, bro."

"We'll see." Sin forced the nagging suspicion that his brother was right to the back of his mind. His hormones were a bit more difficult to control. They were still up front and center.

CHASTITY WONDERED if she was seeing things or if Sin
O'Connor was actually sitting in the castle's tearoom.
And even more amazing was that he looked as if he belonged, in a wicked black-knight sort of way. As her
eyes met his, her breath caught in her throat and the
heat flamed into her cheeks as she remembered their
previous encounter. A sexual flutter burst into life then
winged its way up her spine. Its intensity stunned her.
Chastity wasn't even aware of Jeremy hovering at her
elbow. That is, she wasn't until he muttered something
in her ear. Even then she had no idea what he'd said.
She had eyes for one man and one man only—the most
unsuitable man in the room.

How could she not? Sin O'Connor had a knack for
completely dominating a room. To Chastity's surprise,
he made his brother Harrison almost fade into the
background. Before she'd met Sin, she would have
thought that was impossible. Harrison was one of
those men whose stunning good looks and very urban-
ity made him instantly memorable. Looking from one
brother to the other Chastity realized that compared to
Sin, Harrison's energy and spirit was more subtle, less
overtly dynamic, less...sexual? *Oh, my!* Chastity
couldn't picture Harrison exploding into jaw-dropping
motion, but she could definitely picture Sin. The very
thought of being there when it happened excited her
and terrified her at the same time.

Idiot, Chastity thought, trying to normalize the situation with analysis. Of course Harrison paled next to
Sin, his hair was lighter. He was a warm sunny day
while his brother had all the dark intensity of a thun-
derstorm.

As she watched, Sin ran his tongue over his lips. She
could feel the movement in every nerve of her body,
standing the fine hairs on her arms at attention. She
continued to follow Sin's action before dropping her

gaze in confusion. Unfortunately her gaze only dropped far enough to concentrate on the tuft of dark hair that curled over the top of his white T-shirt. She wondered what it would feel like against her skin, against her breasts. Would it be as wiry as it looked, tickling first, then exciting? Or was it soft and smooth? Chastity pushed the curling tendrils of her own hair back, attempting to tuck the escaping wisps behind her ears. Lord, what was wrong with her? She was standing in the middle of the tearoom having sexual fantasies about a man who was a perfect pain in the derriere. She'd said Sin was a menace. Now she really believed it.

"...like to sit down?"

As if swatting away a fly, Chastity batted at her ear as Jeremy's whispering voice interrupted her thoughts. She had a hard time pulling her gaze from Sin, but finally managed it. Glancing to her left she said, "What?"

"Brigit's fiancé is waving us over. I suppose it would be rude not to join him. Which is a pity, as I'd wanted to discuss my newest theory with you. I'm really excited about it. I'm thinking of writing it up for—"

"Yes, Jeremy. I'm very interested of course, but I agree it would be rude to ignore Harrison." Glancing around the tearoom, Chastity realized it would be almost a slap in the face to sit anywhere else. Especially with old Mrs. Merton casting an avid eye over the scene. The woman's nose was practically twitching. Obviously, Mrs. Merton sensed some juicy gossip in the making, although how she always knew when something was afoot Chastity had no idea.

There was no hope for it. Chastity let Jeremy grasp her elbow and they started across the room. The closer she got to the two men at the table, the more she felt she'd entered into a place with no rules, no boundaries.

One more step and she was afraid she would leave all she'd known behind her. Which only proved that Sin O'Connor was a menace. A menace to her natural sensibility. What was the man after all but some... some...handsome sexy devil who'd butted into her life when she wasn't looking. Surely if she'd only apply a bit of judicious thought she'd realize how perfect her life was at the moment. She'd revel in it instead of letting this man stir up longings she'd no idea she'd ever had. Now was the time to take control of her fantasies, and she'd do it if it killed her!

"Chastity, hello. I had no idea you were coming up here this afternoon. Is Brigit expecting you?"

Chastity pulled her best company manners together and responded to Harrison's comment. "Not exactly. I mean I might have mentioned it, the tea that is, but—" *Great, I'm babbling* "—Jeremy thought it would be a lovely idea to come for tea. Such lovely tea here." She tried to avoid Sin's heated gaze and the mobile curves of his tempting mouth. She peeked at Jeremy instead, hoping to find reinforcement...at least some equilibrium. "Jeremy's full of lovely ideas, aren't you?" Had Jeremy's upper lip always been that thin and humorless?

Jeremy pursed those lips as he considered her comment, then said with all the certainty of a man convinced he was too enlightened ever to be doubted, "Your pleasures are my pleasures."

Chastity started to smile an automatic response, when a quickly muffled sound from Sin drew her attention. Her head snapped around to glare at him. "What did you say?"

Sin covered his mouth with his napkin and shook his head. However, his dancing golden eyes betrayed him. He turned his—chuckle?—into an exaggerated cough. With an overly concerned reaction, his brother thumped him on the back so hard that Sin lurched forward.

"Sorry, Sin. I thought you were choking for a minute there."

Sin lowered the napkin, glancing narrowly at his brother. "Thanks, Harry. Nice to know you're ready to jump in when necessary."

Harrison grinned. "Anytime, anywhere."

"Hello, I don't think we've met. You're Harrison's brother?" The polite surprise in Jeremy's tone was very evident. "Did I understand that correctly?"

With a small laugh, Harrison nodded. "'Fraid so. Sin, this is Jeremy George."

"Dr. Jeremy George," Jeremy corrected, thrusting his hand forward. He winced as Sin grabbed hold.

"Jeremy, this is Sinclair O'Connor." Chastity jumped in as the two men seemed to be conducting an arm-wrestling match right in front of her. At least Sin was. "I met him earlier today when he came by to try on his wedding costume."

Releasing Jeremy's hand, Sin said, "Well, actually, I didn't get to try anything on. I was perfectly ready to take something off, though."

Jeremy wrinkled his nose as he considered Sin's statement. "Pardon me?"

Wishing she weren't a lady, Chastity sent Sin a look that should have ignited his hair into flames. It had no discernible effect. "What Harrison's brother meant was I needed to fit his trousers. Unfortunately he didn't have time as he had a business call that he couldn't miss."

"I see." Jeremy was distracted by Mrs. Merton waving at him.

"My trousers?" Sin's eyes twinkled so much that Chastity considered sending him back to where he'd come from, but she didn't have a shovel. "Now I'm wearing trousers?"

"No, of course not. I didn't mean that literally. I meant..."

Sin stroked his chin. "I thought academics were always literal?"

"Only when we meet people who seem to have no concept of reality."

Chuckling, Sin pointed at Chastity. "I'm not the one who talks to a bunch of mannequins in funny clothes, sweetheart."

How does he know I do that? Chastity gripped her hands so tightly she almost cut off her circulation. She glared at Sin. "At least they don't talk back. Unlike—"

"Sweetheart?" Jeremy's brows rose as he pulled his attention back to the conversation, glancing from one to the other.

Sin glanced at him. "Just an expression, Doctor."

"Why don't we all sit down," Harrison invited smoothly, saving the situation with typical savoir faire. He drew out a chair for Chastity, while Jeremy walked around the table to sit opposite. "I'll get us a round of cider, all right?"

"No cider for me, thank you." Jeremy hit his chest with his knuckle. "It gives me indigestion. I do think a pot of tea and a lovely spread of crumpets and jam will hit the spot. That would do us well, wouldn't you agree, Chastity? You know how you love tea." Removing his glasses, he polished them using a cloth from his jacket pocket.

Aware of Sin's curious gaze on her, Chastity folded her hands primly on the table and nodded her head, echoing Jeremy's deliberate tone. "That sounds more than sufficient."

Sin leaned back in his chair as his brother nodded then walked away. He darted a look from Chastity to

Jeremy, then back again before saying, "My God, there are two of you."

Now off in his own little world, which was obviously more important than the one he was currently inhabiting, Jeremy replaced his horn-rims and said, "Two of us what, old man?"

For the first time, Jeremy's habit of slipping into Briticisms, acquired as a graduate student at Oxford, irritated Chastity. "Never mind. I'm sure Mr. O'Connor—"

"Mr. O'Connor?" Sin murmured with a provocative lift of his lips. "You weren't so formal earlier when you had your hands on my—"

Chastity gasped. "I did not have my hands on—"

"Now, I beg to differ, Doc. I distinctly remember where your hands were and they were—"

With a small flounce, Chastity leaned forward, preparing to argue. "You know perfectly well I was taking your—"

"I know what you were supposed to be doing. My tailor does the same thing."

"What tailor?" Chastity realized her voice was rising, but there was something about Sin O'Connor that sent her out of control. She didn't understand it. "You said you don't wear anything but jeans, so how could you possibly have any acquaintance with—"

Jeremy looked from one to another. "Good heavens. What on earth are you two talking about?"

Giving him a brief look, Chastity said, "Nothing important."

Jeremy glanced around the tearoom, nodding politely at Mrs. Merton before whispering, "Really, Chastity, you were starting to scream like an Elizabethan fishwife."

Sin's eyes sparkled so much they almost blinded

Chastity. "I agree, Jeremy. Very rude, don't you think?"

Lifting her chin and looking Sin straight in the eye, Chastity tried to squelch her instinctive response to his humor. Somehow she kept a straight face. "I thought you advocated rudeness?"

"Don't be silly, Chastity. No one advocates rudeness. My mother would be very surprised to hear you say so." Jeremy looked from one to the other as he continued to lecture. "Besides, no matter the provocation, it is not the type of behavior one uses to welcome a guest to our fair community."

Chastity sent Sin a rebellious glance. Sin O'Connor had only been in town a few hours and already Chastity didn't recognize herself. What would he do to her before the week was over?

Sin stroked his chin. "Those are my thoughts exactly, Doctor. I knew you looked like a very sensible individual."

Jeremy preened a little bit. "I try to be."

"If I were a different sort of man, I'd be very put off by this type of behavior. Luckily..." Sin lifted his shoulders in a reluctant shrug and sent a saintly look in Chastity's direction.

Right then and there Chastity decided she was going to make Sin's tights so snug the man would be singing soprano for the next three weeks. Fortunately Harrison came back with a loaded tray before she could tell him so. Instead she smiled politely and applied herself to the soothing rhythms of the teatime ritual. At least Chastity generally found them soothing...without Sin's eyes memorizing her every movement. She was uncomfortably aware of her growing desire to nibble on Sin instead of her food.

Somehow, she got through the meal.

Thank God for Harrison's sophistication, Chastity

thought as he passed around the last of the crumpets and attempted to add some normalcy to the situation. But it was a strain, what with Sin too obviously pushing the boundaries of conventional behavior, and Jeremy trying to appear oblivious but too intelligent not to notice. He was giving her some strange glances. Chastity was now as nervous as a cat with one life left. Glancing from under her lashes at the men at the table, she was thankful she'd driven herself to the castle. Suddenly she was as anxious to escape from Jeremy as she was from Sin. Finally, after nibbling on the last mouthful of her crumpet, she made her move. "Would you all excuse me? I have to see Brigit about some of the wedding arrangements."

Harrison checked his watch. "Find out what happened to her for me, will you? She was supposed to be right back."

Chastity grinned at that. "You know Brigit and time."

"Yes," Harrison said dryly. "I'm sure something very important came up."

"I'm positive she'll be on time for the wedding." Chastity smiled and stood. She was relieved to be going. Taking great care to avoid Sin's warm gaze, which had been growing more difficult to do by the moment, she turned to Jeremy. "I don't know how long I'll be so don't wait for me. Thank you for the tea, though. I'll speak with you later."

"Hey, Doc," Sin piped up. "I'll speak with you later, too."

Conscious of Jeremy's curious glance, she said, "That's not necessary."

"Yes, it is. It's very necessary."

Meeting his hot stare, Chastity felt her stomach lurch as if she'd been without food for a week. *Why was it that every time this man spoke to her she started thinking of writhing bodies?* Trying to escape without looking as if she was running for her life, she glanced at the delicate gold watch on her wrist. "Oh, my. I didn't know it was so late. I have just enough time to find Brigit then get home." She started to back up and ran into a chair. "Oops. I'll um—"

"Brigit should be in her office, Chastity," Harrison said.

"Thank you. I'll find her." Chastity turned and walked as sedately as she could to the side door. She could feel Sin's eyes on her every movement, though, and was amazed that she could even put one foot in front of the other. The man made nerve endings she didn't even know she had quiver with lust. Sin's voice followed her.

"I'll see you about my fitting a bit later, Doc."

Great…that's all I need. Another opportunity to make an idiot of myself!

After a momentary hesitation, Chastity pushed through the door and finally escaped into the garden. Immediately she darted to her right onto a brick path that led her into a secluded area. She sank down onto the carved stone bench placed amongst tall wallflowers. Attempting to breathe, she sucked air into her lungs praying she'd find a measure of serenity as she rested among the bright blooms. She needed some time before she faced anyone. Time to come to an understanding of what this man was doing to her.

Why Sin O'Connor, for heaven's sake? She'd never even been exposed to a man like this before—so bold, so playfully bad, so sensual—much less attracted to one. Nor had men like Sin O'Connor been attracted to her. They liked curvy blondes with big chests, not gawky redheads with big brains.

Breathe, Chastity, breathe. In and out. In and out.

Forcing herself to remain still, she tried to concentrate on the glories of nature around her. Nature was a solace for her, much as it was for the men and women of the Renaissance. It was one of the bonds she shared with the past, this connection to things on earth. This joyous grounding was the key to her personality, she felt. She wondered if Sin would understand that if she were to share it with him. Not that she ever would, of course. Those feelings were much too personal to blurt out to a stranger, regardless of how that stranger tempted her to confess her every thought.

Closing her eyes for a moment, Chastity listened to the sounds of life around her—the buzz of a bee as it supped from a red flower, a raucous squirrel chattering in the distance, birds trilling a cheerful hello. A soft summer breeze cooled her cheeks as it stirred the leaves in the old oak trees overhead, trees that had been here long before there was a castle. All around her was peace and the industrious nature of life and its creatures. Still, Chastity found it difficult to relax. Her eyes popped open, darting right then left. She kept expecting Sin to magically appear in front of her in a puff of smoke—rather like the devil she'd called him.

Every nerve tense, every muscle tight, Chastity felt as if she were on the brink of a great adventure—not one focused on scholarly research or recreations, but one she could experience firsthand. Was this what her mother felt when she delved into a culture alien from her own? When she made the connection to another human being whose outlook and experiences were so different from hers? Breath quickening, Chastity waited for a few moments. When nothing happened, she sighed. *So much for expectation.* Smiling ruefully she got to her feet and went looking for Brigit.

Crossing the courtyard, she headed for a carved wooden door at the far end of the castle that led to the service and business areas. Yanking on an ornate handle she stepped across the threshold, emerging into a dark alcove off a quiet hallway. At least the contrast with the bright light outside made it seem dark as her eyes tried to adjust. Perhaps that's why she didn't see Sin—not because he'd suddenly materialized in front of her.

Chastity might not have seen him, but she sure felt him. She walked right into him. All that contact with his six-plus feet of muscle was like slamming into a brick wall. Both of them were too surprised to say a word for a moment. Sin's hands came down hard on her shoulders as he held her against him. She could feel the heat of him, fire and brimstone fully stoked and ready to blow. As if they had a will of their own, his fingers molded her upper arms, stroking down to her elbows before slipping around to rest his thumbs against the tender skin on the inside of her arms. He turned so his back was fully against the wall. She stumbled over his foot and bumped against him. For a moment they were they were breast to breast, hip to hip.

"I've been looking for you, Doc," Sin said, his tone husky and deep.

The way he said the words conjured up images in her mind. *I've been looking for you, too.* She couldn't say that aloud. Trying to straighten away from him, she said instead, "I'm sorry, my eyes hadn't adjusted to the light. I didn't see you."

"I knew it was you coming through the door. I smelled you."

Never before had anyone suggested anything so elemental, so primal. It rocked her soul. The rest of her body wasn't far behind. Her head lifted and her neck arched, presenting it to his gaze, much as any female animal surrendering to a mating male.

"I smelled your perfume. It's like spicy gingerbread

kissed with warm honey." Sin leaned his head closer and inhaled. "Or maybe it's just you."

Chastity groaned. She couldn't help herself. Her lids lowered.

"I need to taste you." He licked her then, the tip of his tongue tracing a path from the base of her throat to the sensitive area just behind her ear. His tongue caressed the soft perfection of her ear before he sucked the delicate lobe into his mouth. Then he nipped her with his teeth.

Reason receding, completely off balance she whispered, "Oh, my." She arched into him, feeling all of his muscles tense against her. His hands left her arms and slipped around her waist. Spreading his legs wide, he pulled her between them, his hands sliding down to cup her buttocks and urge her against him.

He was hard. So hard.

Inhibitions gone, she raised up on her toes so she could feel him more completely as his hot hands kneaded her buttocks. With an instinctive movement she rocked forward, rubbing against him, letting him burn through the flimsy summer fabric of her dress. *He feels so good.* She couldn't remember when anything had felt this good. She wanted more.

His lips nibbled little kisses along her jawline, then down her neck again to the tiny buttons that guarded her breasts. Keeping her firmly arched against him with one hand, he lifted the other and went straight for the pearl buttons. As he pushed each one through the buttonhole, his tongue stroked the bit of skin revealed.

"You taste delicious."

Boldly she leaned forward to press a kiss in the hollow of his throat. That same hollow she'd noticed earlier. Her question was answered. His hair was wiry, electrically charged…guaranteed to excite. "So do you." She could scarcely breathe as she pulled the neck of his T-shirt down. The edge of the precipice got closer. One more step and she'd be flying! One more step and she'd be lost.

Lost!

It wasn't Chastity's policy to be lost. She preferred control to chaos. It was how she made sense of her world. The mists of desire started to clear. Little by little she became completely aware of what she was doing and where it might lead...to the very chaos she repudiated. *Good lord, I'm practically making love with a man I just met in the middle of a hallway!* Some of her awareness was coming from the banging sounds now ringing in her ears. Not the banging of her heart, though. Instead a faint metallic clang of pots and pans echoed from the kitchen farther down the corridor. Her vision cleared.

"Doc?"

Ignoring Sin's murmur, Chastity loosened her grip on his T-shirt and withdrew her other hand from his hair. As she folded back into herself, she felt a sense of loss, like a child after the birthday party was over. She didn't know where to look. She couldn't meet his eyes. She couldn't answer the question in them, nor could she risk being tempted by him again.

"What's wrong?" His words whispered into the curling tendrils along her temple, stirring shivers as they passed.

"I don't know what's gotten into me. I've never behaved—"

He dropped a kiss onto her nose. "You don't need to tell me that."

"It's true."

He smiled and loosened his arms reluctantly, allowing her to back up. "I know it is."

Patting her hair and trying to right her clothes, Chastity stared at the tiled floor. "I don't know what you must think of me."

He pushed a curl behind her ear. "That makes two of us. I don't know what I think of you, either."

Startled, Chastity met his gaze. "You don't?"

"No."

"Nor do I." She stared at him for a moment longer before hurrying to explain, "Know what I think of you, I mean, not me."

"You're the most unusual woman I've ever met." He frowned and rubbed his forehead. "I'm not sure I like it."

"I agree."

Sin narrowed his eyes, considering her. "What're we gonna do about it?"

"Nothing. We're two ships passing in the night."

Groaning, he waved his hand. "Oh, please, not an old worn-out analogy."

"I can't think of anything else to make the point." So much for being such a brilliant scholar, Chastity thought.

"The point being?"

"It's a one-moment-in-time thing. We won't even think about any of this tomorrow."

Sin grinned, the white flash of his teeth almost savage in the shadowy hall. "You think so, do you? Okay, Doc. Look me in the eyes and say you don't want me...won't think of me and that'll be the end of it."

Meeting Sin's gaze, Chastity hoped she could keep her thoughts hidden from him. "I, um... I'm not sure I..." Her lying words trailed off as she glanced away, finishing the truth in her mind. *I do want you. I'm just scared to death of it.*

She threw her shoulders back and tried to protect herself by donning a dignified academic presence. She called on cool reason. "We don't even know each other. We're from completely different worlds."

Sin grabbed her wrist, his impulsive movement startling her. "Well, maybe we should get to know each other. I'm here for a week."

"I don't know that that's necessary." She should have known it would make no difference to him.

"Come on, Doc. Where's your sense of adventure?"

"What's the point? I mean, you'll be gone right after the wedding...."

"My brother is marrying your best friend."

"So?"

"So maybe we should be friendly. For their sakes."

"I don't know." Chastity twisted her fingers together trying to hold herself on a determined course of action when everything inside urged her to leap off the cliff and see if she could fly.

Sin moved toward her, a sleek stalking move that put her on guard. "I'd like to be very friendly with you, Doc."

"*Hic!*"

Appalled, she covered her mouth as the sound seemed to bounce around the wood walls. Sin's comment brought back her initial panic. Chastity didn't know how to handle this. Their connection to each other so far had been unforeseen, accidental—a response to the overwhelming emotional and physical sensations a wedding can bring into people's lives. But if she agreed to his suggestion now she was making a conscious decision to go where it might lead in the future. Chastity peeked at him from under her lashes, trying not to let the power of his stare intimidate her, or seduce her, either. No good. "*Hic!*"

Sin chuckled. "What do you think, Doc?"

"Don't call me Doc...*hic!*" It was the only thing she

could think to say as she struggled to subdue her idiotic hiccups.

With a gentle finger, he stroked the outline of her jaw. "You and me. It might be fun."

"Fun," she repeated, sounding like a parrot.

"You know what fun is, don't you, Doc?"

She jerked away from his hand. "Of course I do."

"You wanna try it?"

"With you—*hic*—you mean?"

Sin's voice got even lower, sexier, if that was possible. "You and me together. Laughing, talking…"

Loving? Her cheeks flamed at the thought. Don't be absurd, she scolded herself. As if she hadn't been standing here for the past five minutes doing that very thing. Chastity met his eyes then, imagining she saw devils dancing in the gold depths.

"Do you always get your own way?"

Sin grinned. "Always."

"Hic." Damn the man. Why did he have to be so charming while he was being obnoxious? She pressed her lips together and took stock of him from his come-hither smile to his booted feet. No. His charm might work with other women, but it wouldn't work with Chastity Goodwin, Ph.D. She took a deep breath, then said in her firmest tone, "Not this time. And not this woman."

With a joyous whoop Sin hugged her. "Damn, Doc. This is gonna be fun!"

"I don't want anything more to do with you…of a personal nature, that is."

He lifted her up and spun her around in a circle. "A challenge. I love a challenge."

Mind spinning, curls and dress whirling, she demanded, "Stop this. Put me down."

He held her tightly against him. "Are you going to run if I do?"

Struggling to ignore the warmth of his body, she dangled, toes barely touching the tiles. "What do you think?" *Chastity*, she thought hearing her saucy tone, *what are you doing?* Of course she was going to run if she knew what was good for her.

Sin placed her on the ground and looked down at her. "A challenge isn't any good if you can overcome it too easily."

Chastity could read the determination in his eyes. She managed to put some air between their bodies. She rebuttoned the neckline of her dress. "Some challenges will remain just that."

"Not to my way of thinking. Challenges are the reason people go on. Why they go forward regardless of the obstacles."

"The way you talk it sounds like life is a race to the finish line."

"Isn't it?"

"Well…"

"In the end it's all about how you play the game, Doc." Stepping back, he propped himself against the wall again and grinned. "I play games very well."

"I've noticed." He might be playing games with her, but she wouldn't allow him to win. Not on his terms, anyway. "Okay, then. It's every man for himself."

"Be warned." Sin winked. "It's every woman, too, sweetheart."

"*Hic…hic.*" The way he said it made it very clear that he expected to come out on top in their tussle.

"Chastity, honest to Pete, I can hear you hiccuping all the way down the hall." Laughing, Brigit whipped around the edge of the hall corridor to emerge into the alcove. She skidded to a stop. "Whoops. Sorry, I didn't— Oh, hello, Sin." She sent a shrewd glance from one to the other. "Am I interrupting anything? Because

I can go back to my office and make more noise coming up the hall.''

Folding his arms, Sin made himself more comfortable. "No, little sis, you're not interrupting anything.''

Brigit snapped her fingers. "Damn.''

"I was on my way to see you, Brigit.'' Chastity worried a button, suddenly aware that it was still unfastened. Her voice bobbled as she tried to fasten her dress without her friend noticing. "When I—I ran into Sin here.''

"Literally,'' Sin added smoothly.

Brigit's eyes snapped with humor and curiosity. "Oh.''

Chastity knew by the look in her friend's eyes that she had as much chance of keeping what had happened with Sin quiet as she had of not turning thirty on her next birthday. Helplessly, she stared at Brigit, praying she'd drop the subject or else come to her rescue and get her out of the situation. Rescue came from an unexpected source.

Sin pushed away from the wall and said, "I'm sure you ladies have things to discuss.''

Chastity jumped on that. "About the wedding. Yes.''

"Whose wedding?'' Brigit piped up.

He turned at the doorway and sent his almost-sister-in-law a firm look. "Don't get any ideas, Brigit.''

Brigit grinned. "Right.''

"I still have to try on my wedding costume, Doc. I'll give you a call tomorrow, okay?''

"That won't be necessary. I'm sure it will fit.''

"Don't relax your fashion standards on my account. It's my brother's wedding, remember.''

"How could I forget?''

Sin blew her a kiss and strolled to the door. "I have no idea.''

For a moment after he left, silence reigned, but Chastity knew the reprieve wouldn't last long. If she was lucky, she might make her escape before she had to talk to Brigit about something she didn't truly understand. She backed up, saying, "I have to go. Father's waiting. And I have to work on Harrison's wedding doublet tonight."

Brigit shook her head. "Oh, no, you don't. If you think you're going to get out of here without explaining what the two of you were doing a few minutes ago—and don't try to tell me you weren't doing anything because your hair looks like a duck has been walking through it, your lipstick's gone and you've buttoned your buttons wrong—you've got another think coming." Brigit walked up to Chastity and poked her in the arm. "Tell."

"There's nothing to tell."

"I've known you since you came back from South America wearing feathers so don't try to—"

"I wasn't wearing feathers. It was a feathered headdress and I only brought it into class for show-and-tell."

With an airy, dismissive wave, Briget said, "Whatever! You either tell me what's going on, or I'll stuff myself until I can't fit into my wedding gown."

Chastity's mouth opened into a perfect circle of horror. "Oh! Low blow! You know how much I've slaved over that dress."

"Do I ever. You've been poking and prodding me for the last three weeks."

"All right, you win. You won't believe me, though."

"Try me."

"I've seen Sin O'Connor twice today and each time we've almost made mad passionate love."

Brigit laughed. "Right. Tell me another one."

"See I told you wouldn't believe me." Taking advantage of Brigit's silence Chastity turned and dashed out the door, calling over her shoulder, "I'll be by tomorrow with your dress." She took the shortest path to the parking lot, looking around for Jeremy as she ran. Thank God his car was gone. She raced for her own sedate sedan, fished in her pocket for her keys, leaped in and escaped.

5

ALL THE WAY HOME, Chastity tried to rationalize her behavior with Sin. She told herself she was caught up in the romance and drama of the wedding preparations. *Then why hasn't this ever happened to me before?* She'd been working hard and should be relaxing. *Then why am I anything but relaxed?* She'd been intrigued by the differences between Jeremy and Sin. *Was I ever!* No matter what justification Chastity came up with, her emotional response turned it on its head. Not since the sixth grade, when she'd tried to make the most popular guy in class notice her by pelting him with tiny darts from her African blowgun, had she felt so out of her element. The humiliation caused by everyone in the class knowing she'd dipped the darts in a love potion of her own invention lived with her still and she was sure she'd feel something similar when she saw Sin O'Connor again, after the way she'd practically thrown herself at him.

She turned into the driveway of her old Victorian house with a huge sense of relief. Switching off the engine, she sat for a moment, trying to relax before she got out of the car. She glanced toward the charming home she'd fallen in love with many years before. It had belonged to her grandmother, Granny Goodwin— a petite lady with white hair, a gentle laugh and eyes as blue as the ocean. She'd been an oasis of calm in Chastity's unusual life. Her grandmother's house had always felt more like home than the big rambling residence her parents had bought just outside town. Granny Goodwin's house was more intimate, resembling an old-fashioned gingerbread house drawn on a Christmas card.

She smiled and wondered what Sin had thought of it.

Giving an annoyed shake of her head, she shoved open her door and got out of the car. Who cared what Sin O'Connor thought? She pushed her hair out of her face. She certainly didn't. Regally she swept up the driveway to the front walk and entered her home.

Chastity stepped into the hallway, glancing back over her shoulder at the leaded-glass door. Was it just today that her life had changed? It seemed a lot longer.

Walking to the base of the staircase on the right side of the hall, she called upstairs. "Father? I'm back." Chastity glanced at her watch. She knew he was scheduled to work the Renaissance Festival this evening, but as it was not quite six, she'd expected to find him here until then. She took a few steps down the hallway calling his name. Silence. He didn't seem to be here. Not that she was really surprised; she'd only used him as an excuse to escape from the castle.

Trailing back up the hallway, she yawned. The afternoon's heat, plus all the unexpected emotion that had swamped her since she'd first seen Sin O'Connor had made her sleepy. A fleeting smile crept onto Chastity's lips. It was amazing how much turning your life upside down took out of you. Obviously she needed to regroup and relax.

She climbed the stairs to her bedroom to change into something more comfortable than her dress. She grabbed a well-loved yellow silk kimono that her mother had brought her after a recent trip to Asia. Knowing her father was out for the evening, and feeling unaccountably rebellious, she stripped off all of her clothing and slipped into the robe. She sighed as the cool silk whispered over her skin, imagining for a moment it was Sin's fingertips. "Forget him," she muttered.

But Sin was all she could think about.

Unsettled, Chastity left her room and descended the stairs. She stood in the archway of the study. Catching sight of the sofa, she wondered if a small nap would help her regain her equilibrium. A nap in the daytime seemed a bit slothful to her, though, so she decided instead to curl up and read one of her research books.

She walked into the study, or parlor as her grandmother had called it, pausing to plump a pillow as she passed the sofa in front of the fireplace. She smiled at the cozy feeling of the fringe beneath her fingertips, then looked around her domain. She loved the flowered chintz sofa, now muted to a pleasing blend of summer flower tones of yellows, blues and gentle reds. She loved the lace curtains that cast cookie-cutter patterns onto the pale oyster walls and spilled across the gray-green tones of the throw rugs. If her workroom was the place where her intellectual life blossomed, this room was the place of her heart. With that thought, Chastity strolled through the double sliding doors into the other room.

The mannequins were right where she'd left them, as if they'd be anywhere else. She joined them for a moment, an animated accent to the others. Pausing next to a woman in a purple damask gown she said, "Now milady, don't slump. There's a good girl." Stopping in mid-twitch of the skirt, Chastity bit her lip and thought, *Sin's right. I do talk to them.* She looked at the group. Well, why not? They were friends, too. She spent a lot of time with these ladies and gentlemen. And they didn't talk her to death in return. Sometimes people needed to be alone.

Since childhood she'd been forced to interact with all sorts of people, and she considered herself richer for the experience. However, sometimes she wanted to escape into her own rather reclusive personality. One of the most satisfying things about the academic life was the opportunity it presented to escape into other worlds peopled by those whose ideas demanded response, but whose actual voices were silent. One thing she'd learned as a child, voices could be cruel. As an adult she'd made an obvious choice not to rock the boat. Now she was beginning to question the wisdom of that decision.

Moving to the mannequin wearing the groom's doublet, she fussed for a few more minutes holding up fabrics, lace and trims, positioning them this way and that as she tried to find the right effect. No luck. With a humph of disgust, she marched across the room and picked up her new costume book from the drawing board, then grabbed a pencil and pad of paper from her desk.

"Don't worry, Harrison," she said to the groom. "I'll get it right. You're going to look terrific."

Smiling goodbye to her entourage, she turned and went back to the study. With a contented sigh, she curled up on one end of the sofa trying to recapture the peace she generally felt when she immersed herself in history. Just as she opened her book, a cat, black as shoe polish, leaped into her lap.

Chastity jumped. "Squash. You scared me to death."

Squash didn't seem to care as he padded up her chest to poke his face onto hers for a kiss. Chastity opened her mouth and breathed so the cat could get her scent. The silly thing almost stuck her entire nose inside. All animals had funny quirks, but Squash had more than most. "Absurd cat." Smiling, she scratched his ears. "Okay, settle down now."

As if he'd been paying attention—a trick all cats played when they wanted their owners to think they actually listened to them—Squash obediently turned around in a circle three times then curled up in her lap. He looked up at her and blinked his golden eyes. They were the exact color of Sin's.

Will you stop this? Forget Sin.

Diligently she flipped open her book and applied herself to examining the illustrations representing true Renaissance attire. She studied paintings of the men and women of the era, looking for unique ideas until all the pictures started to run together. Chastity yawned, rubbing her eyes like a little kid fighting off sleep. She settled down more deeply against the pillows to read as the sun dropped lower in the sky, moving around to the back of the house causing deep shadows to invade the room. The muted songs of the birds hummed a lullaby, as did the gentle snoring of her cat. She fought to keep her eyes open before she gave up.

SIN O'CONNOR STOOD in his historical powder puff of a room and wondered if he was completely out of his mind or if Chastity Goodwin was a siren sent by the devil to tempt him from his work. He laughed. The idea of Chastity as a siren complete with floating gauzy garments, undulating hips and flowing locks was ridiculous. So why couldn't he get her out of his thoughts?

He clutched his hair, trying to drive all images of her away. No good. The damn woman was stuck inside his mind like flypaper; all he could see, all he could feel, was her. A siren? Unlikely as it seemed, it must be true, even if she didn't quite look the part. Chastity's hair didn't flow exactly...the curls seemed to puff out rather like a dandelion getting ready to go to seed, but he found it provocative, nevertheless. And he could still feel her hips moving against him. They'd undulated all right. He still ached at the thought of the contact.

Sin launched himself onto the bed. Rolling onto his back, he linked his hands under his head and regarded the ceiling. Or what he could see of it though the softening effect of the gauze that drooped over the metal canopy of his bed frame. Grasping at something to distract him from Chastity, he focused on the frilly bed coverings. He stared at the dried rose petals that were scattered on top of the fabric.

With a sorry snort, he rolled on to his side. Staring at the expanse of space to his left side, he muttered, "This bed is wasted on one person." And he knew just the person he'd put in the other side. The thought of her breathless moans and her hot body made his own breath come faster. He replayed the scene in the hallway...her tongue in the hollow of his throat, her hands in his hair, her hips arched against his. Seeking contact with the memory, his own hips rose. His jeans grew more snug as his body responded to his thoughts. He pressed the palm of his right hand against his zipper. Letting his mind drift he imagined her hand there instead, slipping up and down the length of him as he grew. Finding him, releasing him, tasting him.

"Damn it to hell and back!" Sin flipped over onto his stomach, trying to force his erection back into submission. Instead the movement only inflamed the problem. With a stronger oath, he scrambled off the bed, headed for the bathroom and plunged into a cold shower.

Forcing himself to stand motionless under the icy spray, Sin was surprised the water didn't steam as it hit his skin. Was he really that attracted to Chastity Goodwin or was his recent long stretch of abstinence actually at fault? He was a healthy, virile male and it had been quite a while since he'd made love to a woman. Close to a breakthrough, he'd been putting all of his energy into his special work project. Dipping his head under the stream of water, he vowed that from this minute forward, he'd make time for a private life even when he was working like a maniac. Turning off the shower, he stepped out to towel dry and dress.

Bare-chested and barefoot, he was just zipping up his jeans when someone knocked on his door. A female voice called: "Sin, are you in there? Sin?"

"Yeah. Who is it?" He forced down the idiotic thought that Chastity was standing outside the door, ready to pick up where they'd left off.

"It's Brigit."

"Come on in." He wasn't in the mood to make small talk, but he certainly didn't want to offend his almost-relative.

Brigit gingerly peeked around the door, her curious gaze sweeping the room as Sin watched. "Looking for something?" He was amused by her hesitant manner. From what he'd seen of her, it wasn't her usual style.

Still peeping around the door, she said, "Oh, no…not at all."

Sin folded his arms and raised a sardonic brow. "Maybe I should have said looking for *someone?* Like your best friend Chastity, perhaps."

"Now why would you think I'd be doing that, Sin?"

Brigit's eyes widened to innocence so effectively that Sin was sure she'd been perfecting the trick for years. "Nice going," Sin said with an approving nod. "I don't think I've ever seen a better 'butter wouldn't melt in my mouth even if I were an oven' look." He ducked his head to hide a smile.

Chuckling, Brigit stepped fully inside the room, taking great pains to leave the door ajar for propriety's sake. "I haven't the vaguest idea what you're talking about."

Sin considered the small woman standing just inside his doorway. He was beginning to understand why his brother had fallen the way he had—so fast, so hard. This damn female had torpedoed him when he wasn't looking. Innocent-appearing, adorable women always did that. They came sneaking up on you when you weren't looking…when you were vulnerable. Especially when you were vulnerable. Rather than give Brigit an "in" for the conversation about him and Chastity that she was dying to have, Sin walked across the room and rummaged in his duffel bag for a clean T-shirt. He changed the subject. "What's up?"

From the corner of his eye, he saw Brigit give an elaborate shrug before she said, "I thought we could get to know each other a bit better."

He raised a both brows. "In my bedroom?" That got her. Sin hid a grin as the sexy little elf, which is the way he was starting to think of his new sister-in-law, blushed. He'd tease her some more to see if she'd back off or come out fighting. After all, it was his duty. If the woman couldn't hold her own, she'd never make a go of marriage with his brother.

"No. That is…"

Holding his T-shirt in his hand, Sin turned to face Brigit. "I'm not too comfortable having my brother's fiancée visiting me when I'm dressing."

"Better dressing than undressing, don't you think?"

Sin grinned. She had him there; but he wouldn't admit it. "If you weren't marrying my brother I'd have to say, it depends on what you have in mind."

Brigit tapped her fingertip against her lips as she regarded him. "Correct me if I'm wrong, but I could swear your taste runs more to tall redheads than short brunettes."

"Not usually," Sin muttered.

Making herself right at home, Brigit strolled over and perched on the end of the bed. "Pardon?"

To avoid answering, Sin pulled his T-shirt over his head, wondering why women always had to talk things to death. Maybe if he stayed here like an ostrich with the shirt pulled over his head long enough, she'd be quiet and go away.

"Redheads with curly hair and—"

No such luck. Sin popped his head through the top of the shirt. "Is there a point to this?"

Brigit shook her head. "Nope. Just making conversation."

"Why?"

"Because you're going to be my brother-in-law."

Now Sin was really wary. There was a tone to her voice that made them accomplices—he just wasn't sure to what. "Yeah?"

Her face softened. "I know how much you mean to your brother."

"You do?" Unless his brother had changed even more than he'd noticed, Sin couldn't imagine Harry sharing this type of gooey information.

"And I'm sure he means just as much to you." Brigit leaned forward as if sharing secrets. "That's why I want you to do me a little bitty favor." Brigit's expression got even more innocent, if that was possible.

Sin's nerves reacted the only way possible—they screamed! "What type of favor?"

"We have a meeting with the wedding musicians tonight, so I can't do this myself 'cause Harrison would know."

"Do what?"

Brigit rummaged in her pocket then withdrew a small velvet bag. Dipping inside she removed a sapphire the size of a peanut and placed it in the center of her palm. The rock was as deep blue as a summer night's sky. As Brigit turned her hand this way and that a stray sunbeam hit the stone and brought forth a shimmer of light from the internal star. "Will you deliver this to Chastity for me?"

"Is it hers?"

"No. It's my wedding gift to Harrison."

"Then why are you—"

"I want her to make it the key decoration on his doublet. That's his—"

"I know what a doublet is."

"Great." Brigit gave an approving bob of her head. "I'm glad you're getting into the whole Renaissance thing."

Sin started to disabuse her of that notion, but Brigit sped on, effectively shutting him up. "I've had this friend of mine, an antique dealer, looking around for quite some time for a stone that could be set into a ring after the wedding ceremony."

"Why don't you do that now? Why—"

Brigit bounced off the bed. "Chastity wants a unique trim for Harrison's doublet. That's what gave me the idea this might work. Renaissance clothes were always covered with jewels."

Sin tucked his T-shirt into his jeans. "Why does she need this right now?"

Dumping the jewel back in the bag, Brigit said, "Chastity's working on his costume tonight. If she weren't on such a tight schedule I wouldn't ask you to do this."

"Well…" Sin was at a loss for a moment. On one hand he wanted to go to Chastity, and on the other he thought he must be nuts to consider it. He hoped his confusion wasn't showing, especially since Brigit was watching him like a Labrador retriever after a duck. His reason took a back seat to his desire. "I could drop it off, I guess. It's a nice night for a ride." He stared at the window above the bed. The light was fading, but was still fuzzy and friendly. "Or it will be."

"Great." Brigit practically skipped across the room. She slapped the jewel in his hand. "Don't lose it."

Sin fingered the bag for a moment, before shrugging and putting it in his pocket. "Yeah. Okay, I'll do it." He smiled, hoping he was keeping his anticipation hidden.

"Hey Sin, you there?" His brother's voice cruised up the stairs with Harrison in full sail behind it. "You haven't seen Brigit, have you? I've been looking—"

"I'm here, but—" Sin looked at Brigit and grinned "—how come you can't keep track of your woman?"

"'Cause she's too small and too fast. It's like…" Still talking, Harrison walked in the door.

He stopped in his tracks when Brigit said, "Hi, honey."

"Darling, what're you doing up here? You told me you were coming right back to the tearoom."

For a moment, Brigit was at a loss. She looked at Sin, then back to her fiancé. "Well, I…"

Harrison gave them both a curious look, then shrugged. "Never mind. Look, Mrs. Merton is still in the tearoom demanding to see you before she leaves. If you don't come down, she'll be there all night."

Brigit rushed over to Harrison. "Oh, honey, I'm sorry. I forgot about her. First I got tied up on the phone. Then I saw Sin and Chas—" She shot Sin a guilty glance.

Damn, Sin thought, he'd been afraid of that.

Brigit backtracked. "I mean, I ran into Chastity and had to talk to her for a moment. Then I had to settle a problem in the kitchen. Then I had to see Sin about something and—"

Harrison smiled and raised his hands, cupping her

shoulders to stop her sputtering. "Darling, I don't need a play-by-play. I'm not checking up on you."

"I know." She reached up and hugged his arm bringing it close to her breast. Her expression was so full of light and love that Sin had to swallow an unexpected lump in his throat.

"I came up here to ask a favor of your brother." She directed a stare over her shoulder at Sin. "He was already going out tonight, and I had this little important errand."

"Right. It's no problem at all." Sin could take a hint. He slipped on some socks, then grabbed his boots and jacket. Padding to the door in his stocking feet, Sin said, "I'm off. See ya in a bit."

Harrison watched his brother leave the room. He turned to his fiancée. "He's in a hell of a hurry isn't he?"

Brigit smiled. "Could be."

Cocking his head, Harrison regarded Brigit. "What are you up to? What've you done to my brother?"

"What makes you think I've done anything?"

"Intuition."

"I thought only women had that."

"Not when danger's involved. From the look of you a number ten on the Richter scale seems likely."

"Harrison, don't be silly." She wound her arms around his neck and pulled him down to her. "I'm helping."

Only a whisper away from her delicious lips, Harrison said, "Those are probably the most chilling words in the English language when they're coming from your mouth."

Brigit closed the distance and nibbled his lips. "Sin will be glad. Wait and see."

Harrison drew back forcing her to nibble his chin instead. "Exactly how have you helped him?"

"I sent him to Chastity's."

Not really surprised, he repeated, "To Chastity's."

Brigit's smile was so sunny, it almost blinded him. "Sometimes people need a nudge."

"Poor old Sin." Harrison rolled his eyes as he drawled out the words.

"That's what every man says in the beginning. He'll be happy about it later."

Giving her an amused look, Harrison said, "What makes you think so?"

"There's a spark between the two of them."

"I know, I've seen it, but I don't think it's a good idea to fan the flame. Besides, you promised not to match-make."

Brigit only laughed and kissed him.

As she pressed her sexy little body against him, stirring the longing that was always smoldering just under the surface, Harrison gave up. "Forget my brother. He's on his own."

As SIN DREW to a stop at the curb by Chastity's house, he noticed a bit more activity on the street than what he'd seen there earlier in the day. Cars were coming and going. People were outside relaxing on their porches, puttering in their yards or calling hellos to their neighbors. The entire place reminded him of a Norman Rockwell painting. Aware of the curious looks he was getting, he sat quietly for a moment and absorbed the atmosphere, bracing his heels against the pavement to keep his bike upright.

Sin had been born and raised in Boston and still kept an apartment there, so he wasn't at ease with this small-town life where everyone knew their neighbors. The only similar experience he had came from living in his country hideaway. However, there he existed in splendid isolation, far from the nearest town, so he supposed it didn't really count.

Sin turned to stare at Chastity's house, something he hadn't done earlier that day. This time he looked at it professionally, as a designer might, studying the environment for clues to the owner's personality. He wasn't surprised to see how well this house fit her. Her traditionalism and love of antiquity was matched by the time-worn brick exterior and the multipaned casement windows, which were set off by black louvered shutters and decorated with window boxes full of flowers. To Sin, Chastity's house appeared safe and comforting, sitting cozily surrounded by big trees with gnarled branches and vivid beds of flowers. His mother had loved to garden, so he recognized daisies, foxglove and lavender among the old-fashioned flowers that suited both the house and its owner. To the side of the house was another garden area with a gazebo covered with small pink roses that rambled all over the lattice, scenting the air with delicious perfume. He could easily see Chastity tending the blooms with loving hands.

Yes, this house fit her.

He could imagine Chastity on the covered porch that surrounded the front of the house. She'd be sitting in one of the white wicker chairs with her hair up in a curly topknot, a pencil stuck behind her ear, reading a book. What surprised him was how easily he could imagine himself stretched at his ease in the porch swing near her.

That alarmed him enough that he dug in his heels and lifted his bike to set his brakes before dismounting. He strode up the sidewalk to the porch, and stopped in front of the narrow wood door. With a feeling of déjà vu, he reached for the doorknob, then stopped himself, realizing he couldn't walk in there as if he owned the place. He started to press the doorbell, but before he could push it the door opened and he was confronted by a member of Queen Elizabeth the First's clergy. Startled, Sin stepped backward.

Reverend Goodwin folded his hands over his stomach and said, "Well, well. Hello, my boy."

"Sir." Sin felt like a grubby eight-year-old as he faced this imposing presence. Wearing a white billowing shirt topped with a pleated black robe accented by a wide fur collar and voluminous hanging sleeves, the man was almost as wide as he was high.

"Good to see you again." The reverend added with a sly grin, "So soon."

Sin peered down at the older man filling the doorway, recognizing Chastity's father under the square black hat that perched on top of his snowy hair. The man's dignity and historical costume made him seem much larger and more unapproachable than he actually was. Either that or Sin had a remarkably guilty conscience when being confronted by a clergyman. Considering what had happened recently with the reverend Goodwin's daughter, he was tempted to choose the latter.

"You too, sir."

Reverend Goodwin's grin expanded. "No need to be so formal, son."

Son. It was a common term from an older man to a younger, but for some reason Sin felt as if he were sticking his head into a noose. He wanted to run his finger around his neckline, but he took a deep breath instead. "Right."

"Looking for Chastity, are you?"

Nope. Looking to deflower Chastity, sir. Where did that thought come from? Could the reverend read the guilt on his face? He hoped not. However, the way the man's eyes were gleaming, Sin had a feeling the reverend Goodwin knew exactly what he was thinking. "Yes, but only because Brigit sent me over. Not because I want to—" Feeling like an idiot, Sin swallowed the rest of his words. *Make love to her until neither of us can see straight!*

"Brigit sent you?"

Sin shoved his hands in his pockets. "I have to give your daughter something from Brigit for my brother's wedding outfit."

Reverend Goodwin's smile expanded, if that was possible. "How lovely of Brigit."

Sin cocked his head. What had the man meant by that? The tone of his voice held a knowledge that went far beyond the current conversation. Had Sin missed something? "Is your daughter here?"

"Oh, yes." Reverend Goodwin stepped onto the porch. "Forgive my bad manners for leaving, but I'm working the festival until late tonight. I had a crisis with one of my parishioners this afternoon and now I'm a bit late. You go right inside and see Chastity."

"Where is she?"

Reverend Goodwin stepped around Sin onto the porch. "She's dozing on the sofa. I didn't have the heart to disturb her, so please tell her I had to leave."

"I don't want to bother her if she's sleeping." Sin started to turn and step backward only to be halted by the reverend's firm hand in his back which propelled him back toward the door.

"It's time for her to wake up, Sin. I'll leave that in your hands, shall I?"

Sin glanced at him over his shoulder. Again he felt as if he were missing a part of the conversation as Reverend Goodwin stared at him, his blue gaze suddenly fierce. With a confused shrug, Sin finally said, "Sure. You can count on me."

Reverend Goodwin patted him on the shoulder. "I

knew that the minute I met you, son. You'll find Chastity in the study." Without another word the reverend walked away, leaving Sin standing at the entrance.

Sin stepped over the threshold and pulled the door closed behind him. The hallway was so still he could hear the ticking of the grandfather clock in the hallway. It was as if the house were waiting for something. The light pinkened as the sun dropped in the sky, emphasizing the anticipation.

He watched the setting sun reflect on the white walls—the magic hour…that perfect light only found at dawn and dusk. The time that renewed the spirit and made everything seem enchanted, yet completely possible. Fanciful or not, he could swear he could feel the magic creeping into him. Preparing him for—what?

He walked to the archway into the study. Pausing, he realized the room seemed different to him than it had that afternoon. It seemed more lyrical and welcoming. Now, with nothing to compete for his attention he could absorb Chastity's home. His gaze bounced from the antique writing desk placed under the big square windows to the opposite end of the room where a multihued flowered sofa rested, accompanied by a big overstuffed chair and hassock in brick red, a carved wooden rocking chair and a corner wall cabinet that Sin guessed hid a television and audio equipment. Here and there were sculptures and paintings, books and knickknacks all giving off the same cheerful friendliness that helped create an entire room that was warm and inviting and surprisingly unpedantic. Sin smiled, wondering if she knew how much this room revealed about her, about the personality hidden in the academic historian. Was this feeling of beauty and soul what made her fall in love with the Renaissance period? It wouldn't be his choice, but it seemed to suit the woman he was beginning to understand.

He became aware of low strains of music. The melody wasn't a Renaissance band or symphonic orchestra as he might expect, but was the hot sound of classical jazz. It drifted over him like a rich haze of smoke in a crowded room. He stepped toward the high-backed sofa, drawn by the searing intensity of the piano, drums and saxophone guaranteed to bring his blood from simmer to full boil. He loved jazz. How surprising to discover that Chastity liked it, too. That realization pulled him closer to her, making him even more curious to understand the woman beneath the scholar.

He found her curled up like a question mark on the sofa. With her autumn coloring she resembled a bright oriental poppy blooming in a field of wildflowers, her gold robe flowing over her body like a slow-moving stream. He leaned his arm on the back of the cushions as he settled in to watch her for a moment. Her hair fanned out in fiery disarray over a pillow the color of spring grass. He grinned as he noticed the yellow pencil stuck just above her ear. Curious, he reached for the book that lay propped against her, then jumped as a black paw reached out to slap him. Stung by the contact with a sharp nail, Sin jerked away before he realized what had happened. He looked down at the cat blinking a warning up at him.

"Are you her protector?" he whispered. He extended his hand, letting the cat give it a disdainful sniff. He wouldn't have been surprised if the cat had suddenly sprung to its feet, wearing armor and waving a sword. After what had already happened today, nothing would surprise him.

He wondered if the entire world had gone mad. Since he'd come to town, nothing was as it seemed.

Here he was in a strange house, responding in a way totally unlike himself to a woman totally the opposite of any he'd ever put the moves on, and he hadn't the vaguest idea how he'd gotten himself into this bizarre situation.

He glanced at Chastity, then back at the cat's unblinking yellow eyes. To Sin's surprise, the cat must have seen something in Sin's face that reassured him because he suddenly relaxed, yawned and stretched. Sin smiled. This feline wasn't about to let anyone get too close to his mistress unless he was convinced of their innocence. When the cat leaped to the ground, Sin figured he'd somehow passed the test. Looking at the temptation Chastity offered, Sin could appreciate the cat's watchfulness, even as he questioned his judgment.

He touched one of her corkscrew curls, surprised when the wiry lock twined itself around his finger. Even in sleep she pulled him to her. The music intensified as it raced toward its complicated climax.

Wake her up, her father had said.

Sin wasn't the type of man who ignored a suggestion that went along with what he wanted to do anyway. Staring at Chastity for a moment longer, taking in her shallow breathing and her fluttering eyelids, he decided she was close to waking already so he might as well finish the job. He leaned forward and pressed his lips to hers, letting her sassy sweet taste melt on his mouth. He knew the minute she awoke. She froze like a hunted animal, then seemed to relax as she recognized his touch. After a long moment, he drew back from her, inch by excruciating inch, aching for more of her sugar as if he were a starving kid in a candy store.

Chastity's eyes fluttered, her lashes at half-mast in that twilight between sleep and wakefulness. "I was dreaming about you," she whispered. "And here you are."

Sin ran his fingertips over her lips. "I couldn't stay away."

She opened her mouth and sucked on his fingertip, rolling her tongue and lips around it in a movement Sin felt deep in his gut. Then Chastity lifted her arms and circled his neck. Pulling him down to her, she said, "Take me."

There were no more words. They needed none. Their bodies were talking loud enough for both of them to hear. Only the sound of their breathing broke the stillness as they tore off their clothing.

Sin pressed the head of his penis against her opening, inhaling fiercely when she lifted her hips to give him better access. Inch by inch...millimeter by millimeter he entered her, shivering as her hot flesh surrounded him. Her heels locked around his buttocks and she smiled as Sin surged forward. Chastity rose to meet him. He'd never experienced a pleasure so intense. As his climax built his gaze roamed over her face, memorizing the look of her. His body started to shudder, but he needed more.

"Look at me," Sin said, burying himself in her wet heat. "I need to see you when you come." As he thrust frantically, Chastity's eyes snapped open and met his.

"I'm..." she gasped, tightening her legs.

Sin met her gaze, glazed with desire as he hit his peak and pumped his passion into her equally frantic body. "That's it, baby. That's it."

Eyes widening, Chastity ground her hips against him and found her release.

Eventually, gradually, their breathing slowed to something approaching normal and Sin lifted his head to gently kiss Chastity's cheek.

Chastity murmured, "That wasn't a dream."

He smiled down at her as her eyes drifted closed. "Oh, yes it was, darlin'."

Surprised, she opened her eyes and studied him for a moment before turning her head to look at the fireplace. A blush stained her cheeks fire-engine red. "This shouldn't have happened."

Sin drew back, bracing himself on his hands to lift his weight from her. "Sure it should. It was inevitable."

Chastity began squirming her way up out from under him. "You could be right. Maybe we had to get this out of our system."

Grimacing, Sin sat up, saying, "You're making it sound like we've just taken a dandelion cure or something."

Chastity's lips twitched, but she rapidly got serious again. "Now that this event has occurred—"

"We've made love, you mean?"

Standing up, Chastity refolded her robe, tying the sash so tightly Sin was afraid she'd turn blue. "I think it would be best if we proceed as if nothing has changed, nothing's happened."

"Oh, yeah?" Sin zipped his jeans. "Things have changed."

"Yes. We have this...this...attraction out of our system now and—"

Sin laughed. "Speak for yourself, Doc."

Startled, Chastity turned to face him. "What?"

"I don't think it's going to be that easy to forget."

"I'm not suggesting it's going to be easy, I just think—"

Sin stepped forward and tucked a curl behind her ear. "Anybody ever tell you, you think too much?"

Moving aside, Chastity said, "No, never."

"They should have." Sin ran his finger down her arm, smiling as she shivered. "Sometimes feeling is better." He wanted her again.

Hugging herself, Chastity avoided his gaze. "I've done all the feeling I'm going to do for one day, thank you."

Sin watched her, closely. "Yeah. Today's been kinda unusual, don't ya think?"

Chastity walked across the room, muttering, "You can say that again."

"What should we do about it?"

"You asked me that before, remember?"

Sin arched a brow. "Yep. You started babbling about boats."

"I wasn't talking about—" She stopped and held up her hand, saying forcefully, "I'm not going to let you distract or confuse me again. I don't know myself when you're around."

Leaning forward, Sin studied the woman standing on the other side of the sofa. "I confuse you?"

"Yes."

"Good...'cause you confuse me, too."

Chastity snapped him a look, then pulled her gaze from his. She shifted from side to side, the silence lengthening before she finally said, "How'd you get in here anyway?"

"Your father let me in."

Her eyes grew round as dinner plates. "My *father* let you in?"

Sin grinned his most wicked grin. "Uh-huh. Right after he told me you were sleeping and ordered me to kiss you awake."

Gasping, her hand raced to her throat. "He never!"

"Well, something like that."

"Why would he?"

Sin shrugged and stood up. "I dunno, but dressed the way he was, I sure wasn't going to ignore him. It might have put my immortal soul in peril."

Chastity scowled. "I think it's too late."

He moved toward her, stalking her like a determined cat after a feisty mouse. "It's never too late for redemption, milady."

Awkwardly, Chastity backed up. "Will you please stop flirting with me."

Sin continued to move forward. "I don't think I can. I've had a taste of you. I want more." But next time he intended to savor her like a long-lasting sweet.

Groaning, she walked around the room to the desk by the window. "This isn't fair. My life is just the way I want it. I don't need any complications."

"Me, either," he agreed, following her.

"Then go away."

Sin hitched his hip onto the edge of the desk to sit casually swinging his leg as he watched Chastity. "I can't. We've got a wedding, remember?"

"Oh...the wedding. That's right."

"It'll only be for a few more days, then I'll be gone."

"Yes."

"Then everything will get back to normal for both of us."

She stopped pacing by the wall to her workroom. "Mmm-hmm."

"I think we should see as much of each other as possible over the next few days to ensure we get totally sick of each other. What do you think?"

Rubbing her forehead, Chastity said, "I think I need to think it over."

Sin rose. "Okay. I'll be back tomorrow."

"No, don't do that."

"I still have to try my tights and doublet on, Doc."

"I told you before, you can just—"

"I don't mind coming over. I like it here." He glanced at the sofa with a broad grin. "After tonight, I think I really like it here."

"No." Chastity looked around wildly. "I'll come to

you and drop the costume off tomorrow. Where are you staying?"

"At the castle, of course."

"Oh." Her forehead wrinkled, adorably, Sin thought. "I didn't think you'd care for the castle."

"It kinda grows on you, I'm discovering. I'll see you tomorrow about ten o'clock, okay?"

Chastity hesitated before hunching her shoulders, "All right."

Nodding, Sin turned and walked toward the door. Snapping his fingers, he stopped in the archway. "I almost forgot." He dug in his pocket and pulled out the velvet bag. He held it out to Chastity. "Here. This is why I came over here tonight."

"What is it?"

"It's for Harry's doublet. Brigit said you positively had to have this tonight."

Astonished, Chastity took the bag and dumped the sapphire into the palm of her hand. "Why would she say that?"

Sin scratched his head. "Something about your wanting the perfect trim, so she decided on using this."

"It's the first I've heard of it," Chastity muttered. Her face changed, as if a lamp switched on. "Oh, wait 'til I get my hands on her." Sin sauntered to the door, with Chastity in hot pursuit. "Brigit really sent you over here?"

"Yep. Then your father sent me inside." Sin watched Chastity's temper boil until it bubbled over.

Slapping her hand against the wall, she almost had steam coming out of her ears. "First my best friend, then my father...is there anyone who isn't trying to push me into bed with you?"

"Jeremy, I'll bet." Sin laughed and opened the door,

saying over his shoulder in a dry tone, "But after tonight, he's out of luck. I don't share."

"Share? Oh my God!"

Sin closed the door behind him, but not before he
heard Chastity hiccup.

6

FEELING LIKE A tasty tidbit tied to the stake for a starving dragon, Chastity stood in the parking lot of the castle and looked up at it as if she'd never seen the place before.

She hadn't.

At least she hadn't seen it knowing that Sin was in there. Knowing that she'd made love with a complete stranger, or almost a stranger—a man she'd known for barely a day! If she closed her eyes she could still feel him against her, the spicy smell of his aftershave, his hard hands, the hot length of him as he'd made her feel more like a woman than any man she'd ever known. She wondered how long it would take to forget him.

I don't share. His comment still echoed in her ears, still heated her blood…still confused her with her instinctive response to his possessiveness. Chastity had spent most of the past ten years molding her thoughts, actions and attitude into the image of the professional she'd decided to become. Now, after only one day in Sin's company—in his arms—she wondered why. What did she want from him? Damned if she knew. She only knew it was impossible. They were from different worlds. Under the circumstances the only thing to do was pretend it didn't happen.

If she could.

Chastity stared up at the suddenly forbidding walls of the castle. Somehow this pile of stones felt more intimidating because he'd slept there. She wondered what room Brigit had given him? Was it one of the stately suites on the first floor, or a smaller but equally tasteful one on the second? Chastity couldn't see him in any of the more fanciful romantic tower rooms...her personal favorites.

Stop it, Chastity, she told herself. Regardless of what had happened, it was none of her business where the man slept. The next thing she knew, she'd be asking herself if he wore pajamas. She could feel herself blush as she examined this new thought, especially with her newly possessed intimate knowledge of his anatomy. She turned it inside and out, letting her imagination run riot with the image of Sin in pair of silk pajamas.... No, silk boxer shorts with the thin material clinging and outlining his defined muscles and his more appetizing attributes. No...not boxer shorts. He'd sleep nude, wouldn't he? Completely, totally, gloriously nude. Sin O'Connor wasn't the type of man to let anything constrain him. Not a piece of material, or a woman. So why did she find herself tempted to snap a leash on him? It would be like trying to tie a winged dragon to a lamppost. Wild things and domesticity didn't mix, she knew. But that didn't stop her from acknowledging how much she'd like to try. Even if it was only an academic thought. After all, Sin was a novelty to her. Not as unique as the Boraruendi tribe and their worship of the stinging spider was to her as a child, but close! A smile flitted over her lips at the thought of comparing Sin to a multilegged beastie that ensnared its victims then paralyzed them. It was rather apropos at the moment.

Chastity rubbed her eyes. She should have gotten more sleep last night instead of pacing the floor of her bedroom. After Sin left she had flung herself into work, sewing frantically as she wondered what was happening to her life. How could she have gone from fulfilled to dissatisfied so quickly, which is what had seemed to happen the moment Sin entered her house? How could she have let the devil inside to sow seeds of discontent? How had he gotten into a clergyman's house anyway? Of course it wasn't technically a house of the clergy, but at least one was staying under her roof. Surely that counted for something.

Not seeing her father last night, she would have waited around to speak with him this morning, but she was afraid of what he'd say and what she'd reveal. Chastity had a sneaking suspicion that Reverend Goodwin would take the devil's side. It was better she fight this situation on her own. Not that she'd been having all that much luck so far. Deep down Chastity knew this was only a temporary aberration. One that she would be over today as soon as she saw him again. There was no need for her to build this episode into a story of immense proportions. This was only an anecdote to her life—not the main event.

Not positive she believed her own pep talk, but willing to give it a go, Chastity adjusted her grip on the bulky garment bag in her arms and trod resolutely up the path to the front entrance. Taking a deep breath, she rang the bell and after a few moments the elaborately carved door swung open to reveal Brigit standing in the opening.

A not-quite-successful innocent look crossed her face. "Chastity."

Chastity sent the small woman in the doorway a glance so flinty that Brigit could have struck sparks. "Traitor. Former best friend."

Brigit tried to play it off as she stepped back to invite Chastity inside. "What are you talking about?"

"You know very well what, Brigit, so don't try that little-girl routine with me." Chastity swept past her friend into the hallway, saying over her shoulder, "I put that gargantuan sapphire you messengered over to me right smack in the middle of Harrison's doublet." She waved her finger under Brigit's nose. "And it would serve you right if it dropped off into the wedding cake and somebody ate it when neither of you were looking."

Brigit swallowed a chuckle, gurgling instead as Chastity's look scorched her. She cleared her throat before asking, "How does it look?"

"It looks grr-eat!" Chastity snarled, warming up to the topic. "By all rights that stone should have looked like a big blue blotch at the end of the elaborate gold braid trim I decided to use, but it doesn't. Which is more than you deserve for sending Sin to my door last night."

Brigit grinned. "That sounds great, doesn't it?"

Chastity halted, surprised at the question. "What does?"

"Having 'sin' delivered to your door instead of your having to go out and find it. And in such a yummy package, too."

Trying to keep a straight face, Chastity eyed her friend. "You've noticed his package?"

"Honey, I'd have to be blind, deaf, dumb and over 125 not to notice a man like Sin O'Connor. If I weren't an engaged woman…"

"Well, you are. Remember that."

Brigit lifted her brows until they disappeared under her pixie bangs. "Is that a warning?"

Chastity hunched her shoulders and walked into the great room, trying to avoid answering. "Don't be so…"

Brigit followed, dancing around Chastity like a mischievous wood sprite around a tree. "Can this be a warning from that coolly remote friend of mine? From that renowned scholar and almost engaged to the most stuffy male of my acquaintance, Chastity Goodwin?"

"I am not almost engaged. That's over." After last night, Chastity knew she'd have to end any hope of a relationship with Jeremy. She leveled an exasperated look at Brigit's energetic form. "Will you please stop being such a pain in the butt! Or at least stand still so I can level you."

"Harsh words on such a lovely morning." The deep drawling tones of an amused male voice dropped into the conversation from the landing above them.

Chastity felt his presence before she confirmed it by looking up. Before she could say anything, Brigit spoke, "Sin. Harrison and I missed you at breakfast."

He yawned so widely that Chastity thought his jaw would break. "I was working most of the night. I closed my eyes for a minute around five and must have slept through the chow. I was having a great dream." He looked at Chastity. "Good thing I woke up, huh, Doc? I would have hated to miss you."

Chastity couldn't help remembering how bold she'd been last night as she'd awakened to find him there, her dream come true. She wondered if he would have been as tempted if the situation had been reversed. Looking into his gleaming eyes, she realized he wouldn't think twice. She pulled her glance away, unwilling to let Brigit see how much the man affected her.

"Did you dream, too, Doc?"

She frowned, unwilling to give Brigit an opening for her curiosity. "I...um..."

For a moment Brigit looked taken aback by Sin's comments. Then such a pleased look flooded her face that Chastity wanted to grind her teeth. "Oh, were you coming here to see Sin, Chastity? I thought you were dropping off my gown."

Trying to sound brisk and businesslike, Chastity said, "I have your gown with me, but it's not complete.

I need you to try it on again so I can adjust the sleeves. It's only efficient to see Sin at the same time."

Brigit smiled as she looked from one to the other. "I see."

"Don't you believe it, Brigit. The woman's really here to strip my clothes off." Grinning, Sin leaned over the wood railing and directed a teasing look at Chastity. "Aren't you darlin'?"

Right then Chastity decided to kill him, then cut him up like fish bait if she got him alone. "That's not how I'd—"

Brigit laughed up at Sin. "In that case, I'd better plan on feeding you lunch instead of offering you breakfast."

Sin studied Chastity, letting his gaze travel slowly over her. So slowly that Chastity could feel her temperature rise. A drop of perspiration trickled down the valley between her breasts. For a moment all she could think about was Sin following the glistening trail with his tongue. She was sure her thoughts were showing on her face when she heard Sin's rough voice saying, "Better make that dinner, Brigit."

That comment brought Chastity back to life…and embarrassment. "Don't be silly. It will only take a few minutes to try on your tights and measure your doublet, then you're free to do whatever you want to do."

Sin smiled. "Anything I want to do? You promise?"

Confused, her mind still wandering into forbidden places, Chastity bobbed her head automatically. "Yes, of course."

"Okay, come on up, Doc."

"Up?"

"That's right, up to my room. I can't drop my jeans in the hall."

"To your—that's not necessary. I'd planned to use

the sitting room down here." Looking around wildly, Chastity appealed to Brigit. "Couldn't we?"

Brigit shook her head. "Sorry. I'm expecting Rupert the florist. He's setting up sample bouquets."

"Oh, but we won't be in the way."

Sin folded his arms. "I'm not stripping in front of a florist. Especially one named Rupert."

"He's right, Chastity. Rupert might get the wrong idea if Sin were in there shedding his clothing right and left." Brigit jerked a thumb in Sin's direction. "Look at the build on this guy...I'd never have Rupert's full attention! I'd probably end up with a bouquet full of poison ivy."

"You might get that anyway," Chastity muttered darkly, glaring at Brigit, which was hard to do since Chastity agreed with the comment and was tempted to leer at Sin's body herself.

"Let's go, Doc. I'm expecting a fax so I have to be in my room to take it."

"I..." Chastity looked at her friend, but found no help whatsoever in Brigit's face. She glanced up at Sin, who was smiling the smile of the wicked at her as he waved her up the steps. She saw no way out. "I—I'll be right there. You go ahead."

With a sharp shake of his head, Sin said, "I'll wait so I can carry that bag. It looks heavy."

No heavier than her anticipation. Or was it her fear of being alone with him? So much for the cool collected character she'd intended to present when she saw Sin again. Resolutely she squared her shoulders and then paced toward the steps, feeling like Anne Boleyn. "This isn't really heavy, just awkward."

Chastity climbed the stairs attempting to focus on the wall; but with each step her gaze connected with Sin's legs. He stood on the landing above her—how could she focus anywhere else? His muscular legs were encased in blue jeans worn so thin they hugged him like a second skin. Each step brought her nearer to him...

He took the garment bag from her and helped her up the last step with a polite hand under her elbow. When he touched her skin, she shivered. She knew he felt it, by his carefully controlled reaction.

To avoid meeting his eyes, she looked around. "Where's *your* room?"

"Next floor."

"Oh, the third floor's lovely...the rooms I mean. Not that the second floor—"

"I'm in one of the towers."

"You are? Where?"

"In that Rapunzel chick's room."

Chastity couldn't keep a smile from peeping out. "That one's my favorite." Rapunzel's Bower was, except for the Woodkeeper's Cottage, the most blatantly romantic room in the castle, as far as she was concerned. Sliding him a sideways look, Chastity pictured Sin sleeping in that room....

"I'm not surprised you like it," he responded.

Chastity bristled at his dry tone. "Meaning what?"

"Don't get your drawers in a bunch, Doc. The room's got a feeling of the past is all I mean."

"Oh." Chastity considered the man next to her. "My 'drawers in a bunch'? Where did you get that?"

"Hey, give me some credit here. I'm trying to appeal to your historical nature." He sent her a quizzical look. "When was the last time ladies wore 'drawers'?"

"They still called female underpants 'drawers' in the 1920s, I believe. Drawers were a lower-class terminology, however. Not many people of breeding would have called—"

"Atta girl, Doc. I knew you could set me straight."

Chastity bit her lip. "I sounded too scholarly, didn't I? I didn't mean to."

Sin smiled. "You didn't?"

"Not really. Sometimes I get carried away."

Sin let the silence lengthen as they continued up the stairs to his tower room. They reached the hallway outside his room before he threw a look over his shoulder and said, "So *are* your drawers still in a bunch, Doc?"

"Since I generally wear bikini underwear, it's not likely." Amazed she'd said such a thing, Chastity flushed red-hot as he jerked around, his gaze dropping immediately to her hips.

After a moment, with an effort, he lifted his eyes to meet hers. "You sure know how to make a conversation interesting, darlin'."

Wondering if she could possibly be as scarlet as she felt she must be, Chastity tried to turn the comment into a joke and avoid answering his question. She dropped a quick curtsy and said, "I do me humble best, sir."

Sin smiled, a smile so full of wishful thinking that Chastity immediately felt herself getting nervous again. He reached out to tuck a stray curl behind her ear. "Oh, darlin', if your best gets any better, I might not survive. But I don't mind trying."

She stood frozen as his fingertips brushed her earlobe, almost afraid to breathe. What was there about this man? Not taking his eyes off her, Sin reached behind him to turn the knob of his bedroom door. He pushed it open and stepped to the side. "Come into my parlor said the spider to the fly."

Chastity stared into the room for a moment, immediately noting the bed dominating the center. She then considered the man by the doorway and narrowed her eyes. "You think it's all going to go just the way you want it to, don't you?"

"I never fail at anything I set my sights on, Doc."

"There's always a first time," she said, trying to keep her tone firm.

"I'm hoping for a second, a third, a fourth."

Tilting her chin, she pretended to ignore him and breezed forward into the room. She stepped up to the bed and deposited her garment bag, from which she removed two hangers—one with black tights, the other draped with purple taffeta. She fussed for a few moments, using the time to regain her equilibrium. Finally lifting her gaze from the garments on the bed, she looked at him.

If she'd thought him masculine before that was nothing compared to what she thought now, as he stood stone-still in the middle of the flowered patterns, pastel colors, lacy gauze and elegant furniture. His animal magnetism left her shivering, her legs barely able to keep her upright. She leaned into the mattress, hoping she wouldn't have to move because she might not make it two steps without collapsing. And once she was on the ground... Her thoughts whirled.

Sin should have looked completely out of place; but he didn't. His raw vitality contrasting with the delicate fixtures made the bedroom seem more fantasylike, his surroundings made him seem larger than life. She knew this image of masculinity would be indelibly etched on her mind for the rest of her life. An image as breathtaking in its beauty as the most awesome Renaissance sculpture. Statues didn't capture her eyes and refuse to release them—as Sin did. Statues didn't make her long to drape herself over their cool marble limbs, warming them until they became liquid—as Sin did.

He smiled. That was all, just a smile...and she burned. It wouldn't take much more to make her leap onto the bed and never get off. The thought startled her so much that she immediately knew she'd taken complete leave of her senses. Chastity opened her mouth to say something…anything to break the silence, to quell the desire, when a small electronic noise caught her attention. And Sin's.

He dragged his gaze from her to his laptop computer and printer plugged into an outlet and phone jack across the room, then walked over to the antique writing table and pressed a button on his keyboard. He watched the screen for a moment. "Ah, great. This is what I need." His voice sounded rusty, as if he'd had to force himself to speak.

"What is it?" Chastity asked, relieved that something had broken Sin's spell.

He cleared his throat. "I'm expecting information that I might apply to a new project. My contacts have been doing some similar research in Japan and I needed some input. No sense in reinventing the wheel."

Thankful for the diversion, Chastity leaped into the conversation. "That makes sense to me, too. I always think knowledge is there to be shared. But I've been surprised at how many people in the academic community don't really feel that way. It's as if they are afraid someone will get a bit more attention than they will if they don't hold their knowledge closely to their chest. It's a miserly attitude, actually."

"The old publish or perish syndrome, you mean?"

Chastity nodded. "That's right. But in a way it's more than that. It's the whole atmosphere that you expected to find so open is narrow. Maybe this is just today's academic environment, though. The Renaissance, for example, was a time of great thought, communication, beauty and sharing. Maybe I'm comparing today's attitudes with attitudes that no longer exist. Maybe that's why I like the old ones so much." *God, I'm talking too much!*

Sin hit another key and sent his faxed document to the printer. For a moment he watched the page fill with information before looking up at her. "I don't know if those attitudes apply just to the type of work you do. They also apply to my new research most of the time. I just got lucky with this group of scientists."

"Scientists? What exactly do you do? I mean I know it's something technical, with computers, but…"

Sin swiped his hand over his chin, as if he were suddenly uncomfortable. "I design software."

"What kind of software?"

"Mostly for games and fun stuff like that."

"You design games? For kids?"

"Kids, yeah…and adults." Sin shrugged, a tiny spark of humor lighting his eyes. "After all, grown-ups need fun, too."

"You're right, I suppose. Adults do need diversion." Trying to avoid thinking of the diversion she'd been attracted to lately, she licked her lips and touched the doublet spread on the bed. "That's why being part of the Renaissance Festival is so much fun for me. Once a year it gives me a chance to dress up in all this finery and behave unlike myself."

Sin straddled his desk chair, casually crossing his arms over the back. "Behave unlike yourself, how?"

"I'm another person when I'm there. It's like acting a part. I put on my costume and suddenly the world as I know it falls away."

"I didn't know you found your world that difficult."

"Well, I…" Chastity paused at that, cocking her head to consider it. "I wouldn't say difficult exactly. It's just not always the way I thought it would be."

"Not many people find the world what they expected, Doc."

"I know. I suppose that's why I like to escape to another one."

Sin nodded. "That's what I do with my games, you know...give people another world to explore."

"Yes, but that's fantasy, not re-created reality the way the Renaissance Festival is. You'll need to experience it because there's a difference."

"A difference? Yeah, I suppose. But that doesn't mean one is better than the other. Or that you can't appreciate fantasy and game playing, which are arts of the mind—" he winked "—as much as you appreciate pleasures of the flesh."

Chastity laced her fingers in front of her, gripping them tightly before she said, "I don't mean I can't appreciate fantasy. I'm just saying that I find excitement in knowing that the re-creating and fantasizing I'm doing at the Renaissance Festival has a real historical basis. Someone actually lived it and made it work for them. I find that thrilling!"

Sin's eyes had warmed so much as she'd tried to explain her feelings that Chastity had no choice but to turn away from him so she could continue focusing on something else, namely the purely intellectual and theoretical discussion she'd been conducting. This was a survival skill she'd better master immediately, she thought, if she wanted to live through trying on his costume and get out of here with her dignity—if not her emotions—intact.

Chastity expected Sin to say something in response, but he didn't. In the silence the printer continued running, churning out page after page, the clicking sound adding another layer to the tension that was starting to build again. The tension she'd hoped their discussion had dispelled. Her shoulder blades twitched. She could swear Sin was staring a hole right through her. It made her uncomfortable enough that she considered edging toward the door, until she remembered that they had only four days until the wedding and she needed to finish his outfit.

Taking a deep breath she squared her shoulders and turned around to find him standing a little way from his chair, examining her as one might a speck of bacteria on a glass slide. As he casually unbuttoned his shirt, she had to force herself not to respond like a Victorian virgin. "What—what on earth are you doing?" By the squeakiness of her voice she was positive she hadn't managed it.

He lifted a brow that was only slightly more teasing than his smile. "Undressing."

"Why?"

"I thought that's what you wanted me to do."

"I do. I mean…no, I don't want you to do that." *Liar.*

"You don't?" His smile widened. "I thought you wanted me to try on the doublet." If he was trying for boyish bewilderment, he looked as confused as a fox outsmarting chickens.

Taking a quick breath, Chastity corrected herself, "I mean, yes, I do want you to try it on."

"Then you want me to remove my clothes?" He flicked open the button at the top of his fly, then proceeded to unzip his zipper. The opening gaped to reveal a lot of washboard muscle and a wisp of dark-blue fabric. Fabric that seemed very familiar.

"You don't need to do that. I'm only fitting the doublet." Chastity's head spun as she used up every bit of oxygen to get that sentence out of her mouth at a speed faster than light.

"I thought I had to try on the tights, too."

Her hand fluttered as she pointed at his chest. "Let's concentrate on the doublet first. I'm planning on leaving the tights with you. I'm sure they—"

"I've gotta tell ya, Doc, I'm really looking forward to getting into those tights."

Chastity whirled and grabbed the doublet so she didn't grab him instead. By the time she'd turned back around Sin had his shirt off and had shucked his jeans. He stood in front of her wearing a bit of dark-blue— she could swear it was silk—low on his hips. It left absolutely nothing to her imagination.

Chastity backed up a few steps until the edge of the mattress hit her knees and she plunked down on the bed, sitting on top of the hanger with the tights still draped over them. She couldn't think of a thing to say. She was completely brain dead. Unfortunately the rest of her suddenly seemed very much alive. This is what had happened to her last night...no warning, only breathtaking desire.

As Chastity stared at his body, she realized she'd never seen a man so beautiful. As if nature couldn't believe Sin's perfection, either, a sunbeam slipped in through the window over the bed and caressed his left shoulder before darting down his chest to illuminate his hips and thighs. The light revealed the perfect delineation of his muscles as they stood out in bas-relief against his taut tan skin. Just the right amount of dark hair matted his chest and continued down straight to the heart of him, tempting her eyes to follow that arrow's path. How could she resist? Her eyes continued their journey, lingering on his strong thighs before skimming over well-shaped calves and ending at his bare feet. She shifted on the bed but only when the edge of a hanger caught her did she draw her eyes from him. She reached under her and withdrew the wire containing his black tights. Shaking the tights from the frame she flung them in Sin's direction.

"Since you're ready and willing—"

"Oh, I'm willing."

"You might as well try these on first." After trying to quell him with her best classroom glare, Chastity attempted to keep her eyes off him as he put on the tights. She tried to focus on a spot on the wall across the room. However she was aware of him sliding first one leg, then the other into the knitted fabric.

"I'm supposed to keep my briefs on, right?"

Surprised Chastity looked at him. "Yes, of course. That is if you want to," she added conscientiously.

"It's probably better at the moment," Sin said, with a small chuckle.

It was the hint of laughter in his voice that finally motivated her to stand up and stalk over to him, ready to finish what she'd started—or at least what she'd originally come here to do. "All righty, then," she said briskly as she approached him. "How do they feel? Loose or snug?" If she kept her attention on doing a professional job she could get out of here in ten minutes flat!

"They're not too loose," Sin said. "What do you think?"

At his direct question Chastity had to look. He was right. The black knit clung to his legs. From the bottom of his feet, up over his well-cut calves and thighs to his lean hips, the fabric poured over him, shaping itself to his contours revealing every attribute he possessed. The drawstring waist still drooped a bit though. Automatically Chastity reached to adjust it, draping the doublet over her shoulder to get it out of her way. She gathered the laces in her hands while trying to keep her distance, which was difficult as her knuckles were resting against the hard ridges of his abdomen. She pulled the laces tight and tied them in a bow. Then she took a baby step backward for a better look…and to get away from his presence, which was starting to overwhelm her again.

"You look very nice." What an inane comment,

Chastity thought. Her aunt Harriet looked nice. Sin looked—

His lips twitched. "Nice?"

"It'll be better when we try the doublet." Who was she kidding? The only way this body would look better was completely nude!

"I'm game. What do you want me to do?"

"I don't want you to do anything. Stand there and don't move until I tell you." Chastity reached for the doublet over her shoulder and opened it carefully. "I still have a few pins in the armholes. I've cut this like a jacket, so that's the way we'll put it on. Okay, extend your arms."

Holding the doublet out straight, she gingerly worked a sleeve onto his right arm until it reached his elbow, then moved behind and around him to start on the left. Once around the front again, she stepped closer to work the material up his back and up his arms to his shoulders. She was standing so close that she could feel the heat of him as her hands roamed his upper torso. The temperature of his skin almost scorched her. Her nose was practically touching the soft curling hair on his chest. His tangy male scent reached for her as he breathed—his chest lifting and expanding first slowly and deeply, then quickening the longer she remained before him. Mouth dry, she licked her lips, wanting to say something, but unable to think of a thing to say. A murmur of sound, like a purr under a blanket, came from Sin. Chastity's arms felt like lead, but she forced herself to lift them and reach for his neckline, drawing the material higher onto his upper back and neck. Unable to resist, she stroked the palm of her hand over his shoulders, ostensibly to smooth the fabric until it lay just right. Then forcing herself to concentrate only on fitting his costume, she adjusted a pin where the sleeves met the shoulder. "Is it too tight around the back? Can you move your arms?"

"Yep," he said, proving it by putting his arms around her and pulling her closer.

From what she'd seen of this man, she should have expected him to do that. Perhaps she had. "Very impressive movement. Now does anything feel tight or uncomfortable?"

Sin's mouth stirred the curls at her temple as he answered, "Oh yeah...something sure does."

Chastity looked up. Enjoy this or not, expect this or not, she was no fool. She knew he was referring to another part of his anatomy altogether, but she pretended not to understand. It might be the only way she would get out of this bedroom alive and still dressed! "Is the tightness across the back? Or in the shoulders?"

"No. Not there. That feels fine."

She ran her hands down his sleeves and managed to loosen his grasp. "The arms?"

"They feel kinda loose." He grabbed the flapping front of his doublet. "And what about the front? No way I'm gonna be strutting around bare-chested like the King of Siam."

Chastity considered the item in question. Not that she'd been doing anything else since he'd first removed his shirt. It was a crime to cover all those lovely muscles, she thought, muscles crafted as much by heredity as by hard work. Chastity wouldn't tell him, though. He was too cocky as it was. She only hoped she could keep her breathing under control long enough to finish what she was doing. "You'll also be wearing a big white cotton shirt, like a pirate. It'll poke out of the openings on the shoulder and above the elbow and at the neckline." She reached to pull the edges of the cloth together over his chest, resting her hands for a moment on the material that covered him, unconsciously sliding her palms up and down. If it was possible to be jealous of taffeta, right then she was. She wanted to fling it aside and cover his chest with her lips, first licking then nipping, feasting on the taste of his skin.

"Your doublet gets laced together to stay closed." She strove to keep her tone matter-of-fact. Given the little breath she had left, it was an effort.

His hands captured hers, pressing them tightly, continuing to rub them against his chest. Chastity met his gaze then. His eyes were heavy, drooping lids masking the enlarged pupils, proof of the huge desire that had been building every moment, despite her best efforts. Chastity couldn't give in to it, not again. She'd compromised herself enough already. She'd convinced herself that these feelings were only make-believe. The entire thing was make-believe. There was no possibility of a lasting relationship between the two of them. And she was ready for a lasting relationship.

Gently she tugged at her hands, relieved that he immediately released them. If he hadn't, she would not have had the strength to go. She took a step backward, then another, and finally another. Enough so she could take in the full effect of his splendor. Splendor wasn't too elaborate a word for the sexy devil standing in front of her. The rich maroon fabric made him seem only more masculine, as did the close-fitting tights. Sin O'Connor was a painting come to life...not the effeminate nobleman, but the daring buccaneer rogue of Elizabethan legends. A man whose very vitality overwhelmed those around him.

Sin accepted her retreat with reluctant good grace. "Well, what do you think, Doc?" Metallic threads glittered in the sunlight as he stood boldly, fisting his hands on his hips. With his movement, the front of his tights gaped open allowing the substantial bulge of a well-on-its-way erection covered with navy silk to fill the opening.

Chastity gulped as he posed shamelessly. Unfortunately she couldn't draw her eyes away fast enough to avoid Sin's notice.

He chuckled. "Still think I need that padded codpiece, Doc?"

From the look on his face, Sin expected her to either fall to her knees in worshipful silence or run from the room. Chastity did neither. Walking over to the bed, she unzipped a pocket on the front of the garment bag to withdraw the item in question. Letting the codpiece dangle from her fingers, she said, "Let's see, shall we." If Sin wanted to play games, she'd play games. Fun for adults he'd said. Maybe he was right. This did look like fun.

Sin's jaw dropped. "Huh?"

Chastity strolled over to him, casually swinging the sausage-shaped accessory from its anchor strings. "We might as well get the full effect—minus the shirt, shoes and hat, of course."

"Oh, sure." Sin gulped as she sidled up to him with the codpiece extended and pressed it into position. "Uh, careful. Kinda sensitive there."

"Sorry." She moved her knee into position to gently hold the codpiece in place as she reached around to tie the strings over his hips. Making the entire action as slow as possible, she moved behind him, rounding him like a piece of plastic wrap covering a yummy hunk of chocolate. Leaning into him, Chastity was sure he could feel her breasts pressing against the thin taffeta covering his back as she reached around with one hand to hold the codpiece in place. Her other hand slid between his legs to reach to the front of the velvet pouch.

Sin jerked. "Wha…"

"After all," she whispered in his ear, "we have to cover up the merchandise or every woman in town will be trying to buy it."

"What're you doing?"

"Finding the third string. That's how we keep it in place. Ah, got it." She grasped the third string, thicker than the others. Inch by agonizing inch, she pulled it back between his legs, working to adjust it so it didn't twist and cause discomfort. Chastity adjusted it a bit more than necessary, her fingers bumping the hard ridges and valleys of a virile man in obvious need of sexual release. If the man wanted to sweat, she'd make him sweat. If only she didn't lose control of herself while she did so, which seemed likely given the way her fingers had wanted to linger and explore the very maleness she was intent on covering. Her fingers molded his rock-hard buttocks as she smoothed the string into position, finally looping it over the other two to tie it into place.

She made herself step away then, deliberately taking a minute to get her own emotions under control before she walked around to confront him. Sin hadn't moved. Suddenly she wasn't sure she could face him. She couldn't stay behind him all day though, so she forced herself to stroll casually around him. Taking a position halfway across the room, she could see him in the mirror before she turned to face him. He looked magnificent. He was standing as though carved of solid granite…no longer the sensuous statue she'd first thought him, but a veritable warrior. His eyes glittered, the desire still fierce, then narrowed as his gaze met hers.

"Having a good time, sweetheart?"

Chastity was taken aback by that comment. Not that she didn't deserve it. Hell, she'd even asked for it. But somehow she thought his male ego would ignore her actions and let her leave without acknowledging what she'd been doing. She opened her mouth to speak but closed it again as he smiled, a brief curl of the lip that sent a thrill of anticipation—or was that terror?—down Chastity's spine.

"The next game we play will be mine. Using my rules." Sin crossed the room to stand right in front of her. He stroked her cheek before leaning over to kiss it. Then Sin licked the spot his lips had touched, before whispering, "And I play dirty, darlin'."

7

CHASTITY GOODWIN SAT under a tree in a secluded area and cast a jaded eye over the crowd wandering around the Renaissance Festival. She had a headache. As a matter of fact, her whole damn body ached. The ache originated from Sin. *Original Sin.* She'd never thought she'd compare herself with Eve in the Garden of Eden, but right now Chastity knew firsthand why that woman had succumbed to the devil. And why Chastity knew she, too, would eagerly succumb to him, if he whistled.

She snatched the crown from her head, dumped it into her lap and massaged her temples. If she could just go back a week. She'd be happily thinking about her work, drifting along and dating Jeremy. Life would be so much easier.

But not as much fun! her own devil voice added.

Chastity had been jittery since she'd tried to match wits with Sin earlier that day. After she'd fitted his costume, she'd raced home and spent an hour in her room trying to calm down.

Her head pounded. If anyone had ever told her she'd be taken in by sheer animal magnetism and physical attraction, she would have told them they were idiots. Then she met Sin and all of her high-minded ideals went out the window. Without her knowing how it happened, the man was starting to unpeel her layer by layer.

Where Chastity had once lived for adventuring,

she'd managed over the years to subdue her spirit. She wasn't even sure why, except that adventuring brought change and change often caused discomfort. As a child she'd put up with a lot of discomfort—from other children, from disapproving adults and from the establishment in general. She'd just wanted to be normal...to have a mother who gave her child Cap'n Crunch with Crunchberries instead of dried grasshoppers. Not that it was her mother's fault. Chastity was proud of her mother and loved her very much. But, by God, living her type of life-style wasn't conducive to small-town life. Her mother seemed not to notice the problem, but her father had. Suddenly Chastity realized that was why he'd initially taken a position in a church. Stunned, she wondered if he'd really wanted to do that, regardless of what he'd said.

Little by little Chastity had allowed a veneer of the commonplace form over her life. But now she was seeing cracks as her adventurous child ego peeked out and started to take risks—the biggest one being involvement with Sin.

What in the hell was she going to do about that man?

"Chastity. Hey, Chastity."

Chastity shaded her eyes and recognized Brigit. "What?" she called.

"The afternoon procession is almost ready to start. Everyone's looking for you."

Chastity sighed. Duty called. For the first time in a long time, she wanted to scream, *Screw duty! Give me Sin!*

SIN APPROACHED the tall wooden entrance gate at the Renaissance Festival only to have a man with shoulder-length hair—at least he assumed it was a man—dance up to him and slap him in the face with a rubber fish.

"Good even, good sir. Fresh fish today. Plucked ripe from the river known as the Wash. Done it wit'out me lord's knowing I did." The costumed fellow dug an enthusiastic elbow into Sin's ribs. "But what he don't know, don't hurt 'im, does it?"

Sin cocked a brow and considered the scruffy beggar in front of him. Mischievous brown eyes sparkled up at him from under straw-colored hair that looked as if it had been put through a shredder. After a long moment, Sin said incredulously, "Brigit?"

The beggar slapped him with the fish again, on the chest this time. "Nay then, sir. Me name's Bobbit. Bobbit the Beggar of Boodle."

Sin grinned. "Nice alliteration."

Brigit winked and swept a low bow. "Thankee, thankee."

Looking around the entranceway, which was built to resemble an entrance into a walled city, Sin asked, "Where do I get a ticket to get in?"

Brigit grabbed his hand. "Follow me, guv. A riproaring fellow like you don't need no ticket. I'll get ye in free."

Avoiding the crush of people milling around the gate to watch a mock swordplay, Sin followed Brigit through a narrow door to the left of the huge double gate. "It's always more fun to sneak in," Sin said as he stepped onto a gravel-and-stone path on the other side of the gate.

Grinning, Brigit nodded as she dropped her character to say, "I thought you'd think so. You're that type."

"Unlike my oh-so-proper brother who scrupulously pulls out his wallet at the drop of a hat?"

A tiny smile flitted over Brigit's lips. "Your brother can be very unproper when he wants to be."

Laughing, Sin threw his arm around Brigit's shoulders, tucking her underneath as they started forward toward a charming arched bridge which took visitors from the entry area into the heart of the festival grounds. "By that comment, I'd wager that my brother has been holding up his end in the romantic department?"

Brigit laughed. "I wouldn't call it his *end*, exactly..."

With a chuckle, Sin agreed. "I know what to call it. I used to share his bathtub when we were small."

"What was Harrison like when he was a little boy?"

Sin glanced down at the woman next to him. "How come every woman always asks that question about the man they love?"

"Do they?" Then answering her own question, Brigit said, "Perhaps we do. I guess it's because we're hungry to share every moment that we weren't there to see."

"Especially the vulnerable ones, eh?"

With a sly glance, Brigit nodded. "Women always need an edge, Sin. Especially when they're in love with the type of man who can overwhelm them without even trying." She slapped him with her fish again, reaching across to get him on the arm this time. "That means men like Harrison...and you, in case you're wondering."

You wouldn't have known it earlier today, Sin thought as the vision of a curly red-haired she-devil named Chastity raced though his mind. She'd had an edge this morning all right. Such an edge that Sin was here determined to turn the tables. At least that's what he was telling himself. It wasn't because he needed to see her or anything. Just because she'd given him a hard-on the size of Montana earlier today, that didn't mean he still ached for her. It only meant—

"Unhand that beggar," a deep voice commanded, interrupting Sin's thoughts. Sin glanced to his left, not surprised to see his brother striding across the bridge toward them. What did surprise him however was seeing his brother in full Renaissance regalia. His black cloak billowed as the breeze caught it and swept it back to reveal the severely cut black costume underneath. By the chains draped over his arm and the key around his neck, Harrison was obviously portraying the sheriff of the village out to apprehend a felon.

"That beggar is wanted for poaching." Harrison strode up and plucked Brigit from under Sin's arm. "Now then, thief. I've got you, and you won't get away from me this time." With that the fun started.

To Sin's amusement the two of them engaged in a stirring tussle of words that had the gathering crowd laughing and taking sides before they were finished. Sin studied Harrison, wondering what had come over him. Although his brother had been used to the spotlight as an athlete, this was the first time he'd exhibited any acting ability. Not that Sin was really surprised. Harrison had always had the facility of being able to turn a situation to his advantage without anyone ever minding his actions. Now that Sin thought about it, if that didn't require acting talent, he didn't know what did.

Faced with a Midas-touch brother, Sin had rebelled by being the bad boy every chance he could, delighting in the uproar he'd caused. The majority of his actions were either censored or ignored with a sympathetic he'll-grow-out-of-it shrug. Then Sin discovered a way to surpass his brother, his critics and all the parents who tried to shield their impressionable daughters from his brand of charm and sex appeal. First Sin buried himself in creative pursuits, then discovered technology and finally married the two of them together. Here, in the worlds he created, he could engineer his destiny without worrying or involving anyone else. At least he could do that until he became very successful and suddenly had a company of people depending on him. Firm words from his brother recalled his attention to the amusing battle of words and bawdy slapstick being reenacted in front of him.

"Enough, thief. You keep a civil tongue in that gapehole you call a mouth." Harrison looped his chain around Brigit's waist, and clipped the other end of it around his wrist. "There. Let's see how many fish you'll catch now when your betters aren't looking."

Sin grinned. "That's one way of making sure your future wife behaves herself."

Harrison winked. "Remember this trick, Sin. You might need it sometime." After Harrison had completely secured his prisoner with an elaborate turn of the lock, he turned away from the delighted crowd making it obvious this part of the show was over. Looking at Sin, Harrison said, "I didn't know you were coming here tonight."

Sin eyed his brother. "I might say the same thing about you. Especially the way you look at the moment."

An embarrassed look crept over Harrison's face. "I just started filling in for some of the character parts every once in a while. Brigit does the same. One day she's a beggar stealing fish, the next a noble lady."

"When do you get to be the beggar, Harry?"

"Never," Brigit piped up. "Harrison doesn't beg well."

Sin nodded. "That's because we were taught to work for what we want early on."

"See anything you want?"

Sin looked away from Harrison to glance around the crowded area. "Not yet. But when I do, I'll let you know."

Harrison chuckled. "Don't tell me. Tell her."

"Her who?"

"The *her* you're here to see. I know you're not here because you missed me."

Rubbing his chin, Sin agreed. "Now that you mention it...seen Mistress Goodwin around?"

"I think she's playing the queen of the realm today."

Sin let out a puff of air that sounded like a wheeze as he met his brother's wry gaze. "Why doesn't that surprise me?"

Eagerly Brigit grabbed Sin's arm. "Come on, Sin. Let's see if we can track her down for you." Placing herself between the two tall men, she proceeded to yank on both of them until they moved with her. She resembled a tugboat towing two ocean liners.

"Where does this woman get her energy?" Sin looked over Brigit's head to ask his brother.

"She eats a lot of sprouts," Harrison replied, with a fond look at his fiancée.

"That explains all of those weeds that were in my dinner this evening." Sin grunted when Brigit's elbow caught him in a lower rib. She wasn't tall enough to do tons of damage, but she sure could be inconvenient. He lifted a hand in apology. "They were delicious, though."

"You bet they were," Brigit said. "My kitchen boasts the best gourmet chefs around, including myself."

"Since I eat most of my meals over my computer, you couldn't prove it by me."

"That's not good for you. You need to take time and find a relaxing setting so your food can digest." The severe tone in Brigit's voice made Sin smile.

"What doesn't kill you makes you stronger."

Harrison broke into the conversation. "Speaking of killing you, isn't that Chastity up ahead?"

Sin chuckled as he looked toward a group of lords and ladies who had stopped to cheer on the participants in a game of spillikin. "Now why did you put it like that?" He shaded his eyes with his hand, trying to identify Chastity in the small crowd of brightly attired women, all of whom resembled the costumed mannequins in her workroom.

"Probably because he ran into Chastity after her fitting session with you," Brigit remarked with a dry look up at Sin. "She collided with Rupert in the main hall. For a moment it was a close thing—Chastity was dropping clothes, Rupert was dropping flowers. Your brother rushed in to save the day." Brigit giggled. "Rupert was quite impressed."

Sin laughed and looked at Harrison. "Better you than me."

"It was the least I could do," Harrison said, with a gracious nod. "Chastity seemed a bit flustered."

"Yes, she did," Brigit added. "So flustered that she tried to put my dress on backward. Very unlike the woman I know."

Sin worked hard to keep his satisfied smile under wraps. Flustered was she? Served her right. It had taken him an hour and two cold showers to calm down after she'd left him standing in his bedroom. It was only right that she'd felt the effect as well.

Just then Sin caught a glimpse of fiery hair topped with a glittering tiara. *There she is.* As they walked forward Sin couldn't wait to witness Chastity's stunned surprise when she saw him. He was probably the last person she expected to see that evening.

Propelled by Brigit, who was obviously relishing the role of matchmaker, Sin strolled along the hard-packed dirt path trying to plan what he'd say to Chastity. Unfortunately nothing came to mind, except running off with her. Which wasn't a bad idea. Sin stepped up to her, nodded at her entourage, winked at his brother and future sister-in-law, then tucked her arm though his.

"If you'll all excuse us, please. The queen and I have a previous engagement." He slowly led her along a path that followed the perimeter of the festival. They walked for a moment in silence, letting the sounds of the musicians and revelers on the main green drift toward them.

Wary, Chastity glanced at him for a moment before looking away to step off the path. She walked into a small grove of trees, mingling with the deep shadows caused by the evening sunshine. "Sin," she said quietly, "What are you doing here?"

"Looking for you."

"Why?"

"We have some unfinished business, don't you think?"

Chastity's eyes widened so much Sin thought he could see the world in them. At her uneasy expression, he decided to put her at ease. He wanted her relaxed and smiling. Then he could take her by surprise later. He found her slide from certainty into confusion very appealing. Unfortunately, this morning she'd proved to be as good at surprising tactics as he was.

"I thought we'd discussed seeing a bit of each other's worlds so we could discover why they were so fascinated with each other." Fascinating world or fascinating woman—Chastity Goodwin was like a drug he couldn't get enough of.

"I don't remember our discussing it, exactly."

"Sure you do. You're just trying to get out of it."

"I'm still surprised you've come."

Sin leaned closer, bending down to whisper, "How could I stay away?" He let her chew on that for a moment before continuing, "When I was a kid, I thought King Arthur and the Knights of the Round Table were it."

"King Arthur was quite a bit earlier than the Renaissance, but they did have some things in common."

"Such as?" He knew she couldn't resist the chance to have an academic discussion. He loved the way her head tilted and her nose wrinkled when she applied her formidable intelligence to a problem or a question.

"The search for righteousness and justice, for truth and enlightenment…and for beauty." Suddenly a bit self-conscious, Chastity peeped at Sin from under her lashes, hesitating for a moment before saying, "I don't think those attitudes and desires have gone out of style."

Sin winked at her. "Desire is never out of style, sweetheart."

"Aren't you ever serious?"

Sin stopped. "I'm perfectly serious."

Exasperated, she blew some escaping tendrils of hair out of her eyes, then nailed him with a look. "Now you listen to me, Sinclair O'Connor. If you really want to experience what I find so fascinating and entertaining with this type of world, you're going to have to keep those sorts of comments and remarks to yourself." Chastity extended her arms wide, embracing the entire festival. "You have to open your mind and your emotions and let it all in."

"Okay, Doc, but if I'm going to really do this your way, you'll have to do the same for me. Tomorrow I'm going to take you to a game arcade so you can see what is so special about my world." He extended his hand. "Deal?"

Chastity put her hand in his and gave him a firm shake. "Deal."

Now he had her right where he wanted her, willing to spend time with him. Time he could use to either figure out why she intrigued him so much, or get heartily sick of her. Or at least get tired enough that he would look forward to leaving immediately after the wedding. He smiled and ushered her forward back onto the path. "Lead on to the sixteenth century, Doc. Tomorrow I'll take you into the twenty-first."

She took his hand and pulled him forward, emerging from the copse of trees into the late evening sunlight. "In that case, Sin. Welcome to the village of "Willy Nilly on the Wash.""

Together they wandered all over the festival. Taking in the sights of the vivid colors of the costumed personnel and the multitude of flags that waved above the public theatre and entertainment areas. It amused Sin to consider the contrast between the visitors dressed in shorts and sandals and the elaborately dressed ladies and lords. To consider the contrast between the scruffy, mouthy beggars and the raucous customers who were spending money freely as they stopped at the multitude of craft booths and specialty stores that lined the festival's main street. From blown glass, to calligraphy, to sculpted garden accompaniments, people pulled out their wallets with an eagerness that Sin found amazing.

Then there were the smells. The scent of newly mown grass from the main lawn mingled with the sweet and tangy scent of the herbs and flowers that grew gleefully around all of the houses and permanent structures in the village. Wafting over it all were the scents of the food—of the huge turkey legs and the steak and chicken on a stick that people carried around and tore into as if they hadn't eaten for at least a week.

Sin handed Chastity a cup of freshly squeezed lemonade, adding a large plate of scones with strawberry jam to go with it. "There's something about being outside and enjoying yourself that makes people hungry. Have you ever noticed that?" He followed a large mouthful of scone with an enthusiastic gulp of lemonade. The tart taste of the drink complimented the sweetness of the scone. "Is this where Brigit gets some of her recipes?"

"Some of them. However, Brigit collects old cookbooks, so you never know what you're going to find on the menu in her castle."

Sin shuddered. "That's scary. I remember reading an old cookbook my mother had and it said something about stuffed sheep stomach...."

"That's haggis. Brigit makes it sometimes."

"Lord," Sin breathed, "maybe I'd rather not know what Brigit might use for ingredients."

"That's probably the smartest thing you've said today. However, what generally happens is you'll never know what it is, because Brigit has a gift for cooking. Everything she makes is so delicious you'd eat it anyway."

"That's because all of you women are so damn sneaky that you make us think of other appetites. Then before you know it, you've got us just where you want us."

Chastity sent him a saucy look. "We do, huh?"

"Damn right. Most of the time we don't even know how we got there." That was the absolute unvarnished truth. Sin hadn't the vaguest idea why this contrary woman was so appealing to him. Which was part of the reason he was determined to gain the upper hand with her, he thought. At least he thought that was why. Seeing her move gaily and graciously throughout the crowd at the festival, never quite forgetting the queen she was pretending to be, Sin was more intrigued with Chastity than ever.

A gong clanged. Chastity started, then whirled around and said. "Oh, I'm late. Duty calls. Would you like to come along? Or would you rather explore on your own?"

"I'll go with you," he said, following her. "Where are we going?"

"To the final joust of the evening. I have to judge the event." She wound her way among the people until they reached the far side of the festival grounds. At the edge of the large oval ring surrounded by a fence, huge horses decked in armor and colored fabric waited patiently while their riders, clad in full armor, mounted. Once in the saddle, the riders unfurled flags to reveal the striking banners that identified each of them as they prepared to do battle for the favor of some maiden.

Sin grinned.

"Going to give someone a medal, Doc?" He followed Chastity the Queen up to the platform, propping his shoulders against a pillar, watching as she opened the joust and bade good fortune to each of the knights. With a flurry of trumpets the event began. The horses, released from restraint, thundered down the straight path that ran on either side of the separating railing. The sounds of the joust—the thunder of hooves, the clang of clashing lances, the ring of the broadswords and the roaring of the crowd—rang out over the festival grounds. This was the evening's last major event, Sin discovered, and all the participants seemed determined to go out with a bang! After it was over, the winner of the joust knelt humbly so his queen could bestow a prize upon him. That done, Chastity walked back to Sin who had descended from the viewing platform to wait at the railing.

He indicated the armored knight now leading his horse away. "He didn't want a kiss? I would."

"Not everyone is as bold as you would be."

Sin grinned. "I've got some new moves. Wanna see?" He attempted to sneak his arms around Chastity's waist.

Slapping him on the wrist with her fan, she said, "Will you behave! I'm supposed to be the queen and we're in the middle of the festival. Honestly, I've never met anyone like you in my life."

"You're a rare event in my life, too, Doc," he said, with a chuckle. For a moment neither of them spoke. Instead they tried to find some answers in each other's eyes—answers too elusive to track. Finally he said, "It's starting to get dark. Anything else you think I should see before the place closes up?"

"How about the chapel? That's where we'll be having the wedding ceremony."

"All right, lead on."

Together they strolled through the sparse crowd to the center of the festival grounds where a small Tudor building sat next to an open-stage theater. The simple white cross that adorned the low steeple alerted him to the activity that took place there. However, Sin was more intrigued by a large enclosed building sitting next to it. He pointed at the sign outside, Ye Old Merry Maze.

"Is that a real maze?"

"Yes. It's new this year."

"I love mazes," he enthused. "I remember seeing the Hampton Court maze a number of years ago. I always wanted to construct one of my own."

"This isn't a hedge maze like Hampton Court. That takes forever to grow. It's more like a wooden puzzle that—"

Sin laid his fingers on Chastity's lips, surprising her into silence. "Hush, don't spoil the surprise." He pulled her toward the entrance. "Come on, let's see if we can find our way into the heart."

"I've only been in here once, Sin, and I think they change it every week, so I don't know—"

"Not knowing is the fun part, darlin'."

As they approached the entrance, Chastity said, "It's closed for the night, Sin."

"Where's your sense of adventure?" He tried the gate, found it unlocked and swept her inside the maze.

"I don't know where the heart is."

"The heart is right in the center. It rules the design. The trick is finding it."

Chastity sent him a teasing look. "Finding your heart is always a trick, isn't it?"

"Not for me...nonexistent, I've always been told."

"I'm not surprised," Chastity said. "Maybe it's because a woman can sense when your mind and heart are focused on something...or someone else."

"At the moment, darlin', my mind is focused strictly on solving this puzzle."

"What about your heart?"

"What do you think, Doc?"

He waited for Chastity to answer, but she didn't. Instead she walked before him into the narrow corridors of the maze, as if having pushed so far, she'd decided to back off. Sin followed her, admiring the way her back stayed so straight while her skirt swayed from side to side. He wanted to bend that straight back over his arm until she conformed to him like a willow to a windstorm as he aroused her to a storm's fury. Trying to keep temptation at bay, he looked around as they entered the first corridor.

"This is great," Sin commented. "An artist designed this, I'd say."

The walls were painted with beautiful brush strokes that turned ordinary wood into a breathtaking display of nature. The hedges were enlivened with bits of branches and flowers to produce a three-dimensional effect without being so elaborate that it created claustrophobia. Here and there, cunningly drawn animals peered out from under the bushes, or peeked out from between the branches. The ceiling high above them was painted to resemble a sky, but only dim lights illuminated the inside. These were chosen to keep the maze more mysterious, Sin decided as he paused for a moment, practically sniffing the air as he tried to find the puzzle's secrets. This was a challenge he relished. Unlocking puzzles, from a computer's pure logical simplicity to people's illogical complexity, was the meaning of life to him. Perhaps that was one of the reasons he liked to design such complex games. At one point he had even created a game that used this maze idea—although in a much weirder way. He started to tell Chastity about it when she stopped so suddenly he ran into her. Taking advantage of the moment, he wrapped his arms around her, pulling her back against him. He glanced around her to see the first break in the corridor, their first challenge. "Right or left, Doc?"

Chastity looked both ways as if standing at a crosswalk. "Right."

Grinning, Sin squeezed her so robustly that she squeaked. "I don't think so." Taking her hand in a firm grasp, he turned left, and proceeded deeper into the maze.

They continued to twist and turn until Chastity finally said, "I think we're just going around in circles."

Sin took her hand and squeezed it, pulling her into another corridor. "Oh ye of little faith."

"No...oh, look." Chastity pointed at a opening up ahead of them. "I think I see an opening up there."

"Ah," Sin breathed. "The heart. I told you we'd find it." He led Chastity forward. The area was hidden by three-dimensional branches. Here Sin could imagine he was actually in the center of a live hedge. They pushed their way through the branches to find the inner sanctum decorated with small fairy lights and adorned with flowers. There was a feeling of reality and fantasy at the same time, a feeling accentuated by the circular skylight overhead that revealed the darkened sky highlighted by the last wisps of day and the glimmer of the stars. A white bench rested regally in the center of the circle where it glowed in the pearly gleam of the moon. Sin led Chastity to the seat and sat. He pulled her down beside him. "Here we are."

"No thanks to me," Chastity laughed. "I kept wanting to go in the wrong direction."

"Directionally challenged, eh?" Sin chuckled and tucked a wispy curl behind Chastity's ear. "Lucky for you I happened along, fair lady." He couldn't keep his fingers from tracing the outline of her ear, from the top curve down the delicate shell, to the plump lobe that begged for his lips. He tried to restrain himself. Then wondered why he was bothering. *See what you want and take it.*

Chastity's breathing increased. "Yes. I…would have been thoroughly lost if I were alone. Someone would have found me in here in the morning."

Sin leaned over and succumbed to temptation, gently nibbling on her ear. "I think this is the sexiest ear I've ever seen."

"Oh," Chastity gasped. "Ears…ears…aren't sexy."

Sin's tongue traced the rim, then darted inside. "Yours are." He switched to the other side by nibbling his way down her jawline and across her chin then up the other side. Once there, he gave it the same loving treatment as he'd given the other one. "What perfume are you wearing?"

"Jasmine."

He inhaled. The aroma went right to his head. "You smell just like a hot summer night in Savannah."

"I've…never been to Savannah."

He closed his eyes, inhaling again, thinking that for the moment everything he could ever want was right here. Senses swimming, he whispered, "I'll take you there."

He cupped a hand under her chin and turned her face to his. Wanting to take his time, he prolonged the moment by staring into her eyes. The pupils were wide and dark, bottomless and fathoms deep with her emotions. Sin knew his must seem the same. This woman caused a depth of yearning in him that was bone deep. No surface emotion this, but desire that twisted his gut. When he couldn't take the waiting anymore he covered her lips with his. Gently at first, he stroked his tongue over her ripe mouth. She tasted of lemonade and ripe red strawberries—tart and sweet at the same time. It was a taste he was beginning to associate with Chastity. He slipped his tongue inside her mouth to explore every recess, and was stunned when she took control of the situation. Her tongue tangled with his…a duel of desire as lusty as life itself. He jerked as her lips closed around his tongue and she began to suck. Every nerve jumped. Sin moaned. He was positive he'd never felt desire this intense before. It had been building since he'd first seen her. Making love to her the night before had only heightened his passion until now it was ready to rage. He withdrew briefly from her, then opened his mouth wider to take her lips again.

He put his hands on her then, no longer able to keep from touching her elegant swanlike neck. He caressed her skin, his thumbs sliding downward like marbles rolling over satin. Tearing his lips from hers, he pressed little kisses down her jaw until he reached the hollow where her life pulsed at the base of her neck.

He cupped her shoulders, slipping up under the lace ruff to find the flesh beneath. Her shoulders were as silken as her dress. He caressed them, soothing and smoothing at the same time. All the time wanting to go lower, needing to go lower, to touch her breasts, to tease her nipples…first with his hands, then with his lips.

Unable to restrain himself any longer, he pressed kisses onto the creamy mounds that swelled above the neckline of her dress. He followed the kisses with the tip of his tongue as he traced the path his lips had blazed. Emboldened by Chastity's soft sighs and murmurings, he boldly plunged his tongue into the deep hollow between her breasts. His hands took the place of his lips, smoothing, shaping and cupping her flesh, plunging into the sides of her bodice to find her full roundness. He lifted her breasts out of their snug nest, until he could see them in all of their glory. They almost shimmered as the light of the moon rose higher to illuminate the heart of the maze.

"I've never seen anything so wonderful," Sin said, drawing back slightly to imprint the sight on his memory. Chastity only responded with a groan as she arched her back to press her breasts closer to him. He needed no more urging. He lapped at first one nipple, then the other. He rolled the erect nubs between his thumb and forefinger, delighting in the little moans that left Chastity's lips as she responded to the excitement he was creating.

"Please…" she whispered.

"Oh, I'm very pleased…" He sucked her nipple into his mouth, bending her backward over his arm like the very willow he'd earlier imagined. Lifting her in his arms, he raised up to straddle the bench, then sat down so he could pull her legs up and around his hips. Firmly he settled her against him, his erection pressing against her femininity, his hips rocking forward to gain entrance.

He lifted his head and met her eyes as he pulled her

higher against him. "The heart of the maze," he whispered, pressing his hips against her again.

"Not yet...you're only at the front door."

He smiled at her breathless attempt to keep control. His hands left her waist to pull her skirt up so he could slide his fingertips over her thighs, steadily advancing to his prize. "Then let me in. I want to give my all for England."

Chastity smiled, the tense smile of unbridled desire aching for satisfaction. She ran her tongue over her lips as she stared at him. "You're expecting a hero's reward? A medal perhaps?"

His fingers touched the bit of silk covering her core. "This is better than any medal, your majesty."

Chastity gasped as his fingers slipped inside the edge of her panties to touch her flesh. "Something tells me your all is going to be pretty damn good."

8

CHASTITY COULDN'T THINK. She could only feel. Feel her breasts rise to meet his lips. Feel the shudders race through her as his finger slipped under her bikinis. Feel the electric charge of his circling fingers as he teased her sensitive flesh, starting a slow building tension that begged for release. She moaned and threw her head back, looking up to the sky as she arched against his supporting arm, feeling as if she could bay at the moon that peeked out from behind a cloud up above her. Had she ever felt this vibrant, this alive? Or had she been a creature of the night before, hiding her true sensual nature under a cloak of respectability and a touch-me-not attitude...taking refuge behind predictable relationships like the one she now had with Jeremy? She hated to think so, but she was afraid it was true. Why this one man should be the one to make her realize it, she had no idea.

Sin impatiently began undoing the laces that kept her bodice closed, loosening the stays one by one until he could spread the front of the dress and reveal her fully down to her waist. She thrilled at the look on his face, at the sharp almost painful pinch of his desire. Automatically she moved, offering him more of herself, wanting him to take her...needing him to ravage her. Ducking his head, he wasted no time. The dress slipped off her shoulders as she arched again when his lips closed over a nipple. He sucked the taut peak until she whimpered.

He lifted his head, his eyes burning as they met hers. "Am I hurting you?"

"Yes...no...oh, even if you were, it wouldn't matter. Nothing matters but this." She plunged her hands into his hair and pulled him to her, her lips seeking his like a heat-seeking missile ready to explode. Frantically she opened her mouth to try to absorb him, all the ripe, hot musky male taste of him. She needed him, from his firm lips to his active tongue, to his hard muscles and clever fingers. She bucked forward, her hips coming into contact with the hard bulge he sported like a medal of manly honor. In Sin's arms, Chastity finally understood the fertility rites she had witnessed as a child when her mother traveled to distant cultures. They were meant to create this bond that took one outside one's body into a realm that was pure sensation. Rubbing against him, she realized that this feeling was one of the most sublime moments of her life so far. She couldn't even think clearly enough to imagine how it could be any better than it was.

Through her half-open eyes, from under her lashes she glimpsed a star seeming to wink down at her. The heavens approved and—as Sin pulled her onto his lap to straddle him—so did she.

But the sound of voices intruded. Softly at first, then a bit louder, as if the speakers had no fear, no inkling of finding anyone inside the closed maze, much less in this position. Reluctantly they pulled away from each other, but unable to just stop abruptly. They continued to tease, to taste, to tempt. Chastity's lips kept coming back to Sin's as the heat of him pulsed against her.

"Please," she whispered, not knowing if she was asking him to keep going or to stop.

"Yes." The ache in his voice penetrated Chastity's desire-drugged mind. She slipped her hands from his hair and down to his shoulders, drawing back to meet his gaze. She was delighted to see that the pain and tension in his eyes equaled her own. She tried to think of something to say, but her mind was blank. Perhaps her expression said it all because Sin grasped her waist and lifted her away from him. She sat back on the bench and took a deep breath, only then becoming fully aware of her gaping bodice. For a moment, she preened for him in a mating ritual as old as time, delighting as his eyes darkened again. Before either of them could make another move, reality and the twentieth century took over. Not to mention the voice of her best friend, Brigit.

"Harrison, what are you doing? It's dark in here."

"That's the whole idea, darling. I've been dying to get you alone all evening."

Brigit giggled. "We can go home to the castle and be alone."

"I can't wait that long."

"Mmm, I see what you mean."

"Besides," Harrison continued. "I've been wanting to do this since they built this place."

Listening, Chastity gasped and yanked the edges of her dress together, trying to cover the breasts that wanted only to be covered by Sin's hungry mouth. "Sin," Chastity hissed. "It's Brigit and Harrison."

His desire rapidly evaporating, Sin nodded. "Seems so."

"I can't believe they're coming in here to...to..." Chastity trailed off as she realized she and Sin were in here doing the very thing her friend and his brother were contemplating.

Sin chuckled. "Great minds—"

"Hush. They'll hear us." Frantic now, Chastity scrambled off the bench and started adjusting her clothing. She glanced up to see Sin slowly stand, as if his body were resisting any movement beyond the one he'd been driving toward a moment ago. She understood his problem.

"We wouldn't want that would we, your majesty." Giving her a wink, Sin adjusted his jeans and tucked in his shirt, which had somehow come undone. Chastity was briefly aware that she had ripped it out of his pants sometime in the past fifteen minutes so she could get at his chest.

Embarrassment rapidly replaced passion. How could she have done something like this in the middle of the Renaissance Festival? How could she behave this way anywhere…much less in public? If she didn't know better, she'd swear he'd put a spell on her. Did devils cast spells? She glanced at Sin, caught by the exciting line of his cheek and the strong sweep of his jaw as he turned to listen to the intruders.

The voices and loving laughter were getting closer. Biting her lip, Chastity attempted to smooth her hair, which probably looked as if it had been caught in an electric mixer. Sin confirmed that when he said, "Give it up, Doc."

She flashed him a look, feeling her cheeks flame. "I can't face them looking as if we've been in here practically making love."

Sin grinned and reached to adjust her lace ruff. "There was no practically about it."

She jerked as his knuckle brushed her skin and set off sparks from the fire still burning under the surface. "Even so—"

Just then Brigit and Harrison came around the corner. As they emerged through the branches into the center of the maze, they stopped so suddenly that Chastity was tempted to laugh. Hysteria, she had no doubt. For a long moment the four of them just looked at each other. Chastity was positive this was one of the most embarrassing moments of her life, especially when she glanced down to see that her laces were crooked, causing the bodice to fit in a slightly lopsided way. She became even more embarrassed as she noticed the top of her breasts swelling from the low neckline. The sensitive skin had been visibly reddened by the scrape of Sin's beard. *Damn!* She cast a swift look to the side to be certain that Sin was presentable. He was—except for the still obvious proof of his passion.

Finally Harrison said, "Well, well, well…"

Chastity could have died when Sin grinned, saying, "I do my humble best."

Brigit looked from Chastity to Sin, then back to Chastity. With a casual smile, she said, "I suppose Chastity has been showing you around the festival."

"I've been seeing everything her majesty has to offer."

Ignoring Brigit's gurgle of laughter, which she covered with a cough, Chastity snapped him a look. How dare he take such a cavalier attitude! She had a reputation to uphold. Of course, the fact that she herself had been one step away from eagerly compromising that reputation wasn't the issue. At least it wasn't the issue she wanted to deal with now. Now, she had to salvage the situation. "I took him around to see all the sights, and he wanted to see the maze," she said. "It was closed, but we came in anyway and we…" She trailed off as she met Brigit's interested gaze.

"We?" prompted Brigit, with a smile.

"We found the heart of the maze and sat down to enjoy—" Chastity winced, knowing Brigit would be finishing the sentence in her own mind and come to the obvious conclusions.

Sin came to her rescue. "We've been watching the sky as night falls. I've got a thing for constellations."

"Ah, yes," said Brigit. "I love how the stars form such interesting positions."

The only position Chastity could think of at the moment was flat on her back with Sin over her. In an effort to get away she tipped her wrist to look at her watch. "Oh, my, look at the time," she said before realizing she wasn't wearing a watch. Now completely flustered, she backed up before seeing that the only way out was in front of her. "I have to get home. I still have work to do on the wedding costumes."

"Wait for me," Sin said.

Looking over her shoulder, Chastity waved a hand in his direction. "That's not necessary. Stay and visit."

Sin laughed. "I think I'm somewhat superfluous at the moment. Wouldn't you say, Harry?"

Laughing back, Harrison said, "Definitely a third wheel."

Chastity didn't wait to hear any more. She took off into the maze and immediately took a wrong turn. She paced forward refusing to stop, because Sin was right behind her telling her to. "Go away," she yelled over her shoulder.

"I can't."

"Why not?"

"Because if I go away you're going to be lost in here until morning."

Chastity stopped and looked around the dim passageway. He had a point.

"Trust me," Sin said, taking her hand and leading her down one corridor, then another and another until they emerged through the front entrance.

"Do you think Brigit and Harrison will be all right? Can they find their way out, do you think?"

Sin grinned. "I don't think they'll much care."

Chastity gave a little shrug, peeping at him from under her lashes. Meeting his sparkling eyes and smiling lips she whispered, "I know the feeling."

"Me, too."

They walked the festival grounds in silence. Chastity wasn't sure what to say. She had a suspicion that Sin was similarly tongue-tied. Finally she said, "I thought I understood before, but now I don't know what's happening here—"

"Shh. Let's not analyze it to death."

"I wasn't going to—"

"Yes, you were. So was I, to tell the truth."

Chastity paced forward, passing the craft buildings now shuttered for the evening. "It's not as if anything will come of this situation."

"You're right."

At those words, Chastity's heart sank. Why, she wasn't sure. After all, she'd said it first. Wasn't saying it first the most important thing?

"Did you drive?" Sin asked as they approached the front gate.

"Yes." She wet her lips, her mouth suddenly dry. "Do you need a ride?"

Holding the door open for her, Sin followed her outside the entranceway. "I've got my bike."

"That sounds like fun." Chastity was relieved not to be alone in a dark car with him. She needed time by herself.

"Have you ever been on a motorcycle?"

"No."

Sin walked her to her car, politely taking her keys to open her door. He rolled down her window to let the heat escape. "How about I take you for a ride tomorrow? There's a great computer game mall around here I've been told. Ever been there?"

"I don't think—"

"Look, Doc, play fair. I came to see some of your world. Now it's your turn to see some of mine."

Carefully tucking her costume around her, Chastity got in the car. "What's the point?"

He leaned on the open car door, looking down at her. "Knowledge. Isn't that what you revere? Weren't the people of the Renaissance seekers of truth? Weren't they looking for information, for the universal order of things? I say, where better to find it but in the purity of a computer?" He closed her door, checking to be certain it was closed tightly. "No. Don't argue with me now. Come and experience it first."

"I—"

He leaned down to look through the window. "Doc, you're not going to dump on me are you? This little date won't be too strange for your historical mind to deal with, I promise."

"I've spent parts of my childhood in some very strange places and—"

"Great, then you'll fit right in at a game mall."

He straightened, waved casually then backed up and strolled over to his bike. "I have work to do tomorrow. I know you have, too, so I'll see you around dinnertime, okay?" He didn't wait for an answer.

"CHASTITY? CHASTITY? Where are you?"

Chastity poked her head around one of her mannequins. "Here, Father."

"I've got a letter from your mother." He waved the envelope in his hand. "Shall I read you some of it?"

"Only some of it?"

Her father's eyes twinkled as a slight flush stained his cheeks. "Some of it *is* private…"

Chastity's eyes widened. "Father, I'm shocked." She giggled at the thought of her fiftyish parents sending steamy messages through the mail. The giggle died as she realized how marvelous that was. In an age when so many people shed their companions, she had parents who were not only devoted to each other, but enthusiastic!

"If you're shocked, my dear, then your mother and I didn't bring you up very well at all."

"Maybe *shocked* is too strong a word." She watched her father stroke the letter, almost as if it were his wife's cheek. "You miss Mother, don't you?"

Reverend Goodwin smiled with a hint of sadness that fought with the inevitable look of pride that came over his face when he discussed his wife. "Yes, I do. Very much. I considered myself the luckiest man on earth when she chose me." He looked up, with an expression of wonder in his eyes. "She could have had anyone you know, but she chose me."

"No wonder. You were a real babe in college. I've seen photos."

Winking, her father said, "I'm still a babe where it counts."

"Father!" He never ceased to surprise her.

Reverend Goodwin chuckled, then unfolded the letter. Pulling out his glasses, he read. "'I expect to wrap up my research much earlier than I'd thought. With any luck, I'll see you in the fall. Give Chastity a hug and kiss for me. Tell her I've seen a vision and I'm sending her a letter.'"

"She's seen a vision?" Wrinkling her nose, Chastity pondered her mother's comment. "I didn't know she saw visions. What kind of vision?"

"Well if it was anyone but your mother, who's out in the middle of the jungle with limited access to civilized amenities..." Her father scratched his head. "I'd say she drank too much native bug juice. Some of it is quite potent."

"Potent enough for visions?"

"Oh, definitely."

"Maybe she has some new insight into the origins of man or something."

"It sounded more personal to me. As if it were something that involves you."

Chastity turned back to one of the mannequins and picked up the pins she'd been using a moment before. "The only vision that would satisfy me at the moment is having these costumes finished and getting to the wedding on time." Any other vision might include Sin, and she'd been trying to keep that one at a distance.

She could feel her father watching her for a moment before he spoke. "Is Sin amenable to wearing a Renaissance outfit now?"

She was so startled by her father's comment that she jabbed herself in the finger. "Ouch...what made you ask that?"

"Oh, just something he said on the telephone."

"On the telephone? You spoke to him? When?"

"About a half hour ago."

"I was here, why didn't he—"

"Sin told me not to bother you while you were working, but to tell you he'd be a bit late...about seven or so. He had something to take care of late this afternoon."

Chastity was amazed at how her heart leaped when her father mentioned Sin. As usual, her reaction was completely out of proportion to their casual liaison. Hopefully she'd get over this tendency or she'd be jumping every time her father spoke of sins and sinners in a church service.

"Oh." He snapped his fingers and turned. "I almost forgot. I ran into Jeremy this morning at the post office. He said he'd been called out of town—very unexpected—but he'd see you soon."

Jeremy. She'd scarcely thought of him in days. She should have. At least called or something. Feeling guilty and uncomfortable, Chastity peered over the shoulder of the mannequin she was working on.

Smoothing his shoulder she thought, at least one man in her life was manageable.

"Anything else I should know, Father? Other appointment changes or any insights you'd like to share? Should I buy a lottery ticket tomorrow or change my..." She trailed off as she met his wise eyes, aware that she'd been sharp and sarcastic, taking her frustration and confusion out on the person she loved more than anyone else in the world.

"Pardon me?"

Her father's gently amused tone didn't make her any happier. His familiarity with both Sin and Jeremy and the careful way he'd tried not to put any emphasis on either of their names, as if he were saying "These two men are interesting and I really like one much better than the other, but I don't want to say who in the interest of fairness" really hit her between the eyes. Chastity immediately began comparing the two men herself. One was so careful and one so reckless. One was so angelically unthreatening and one a devil to her peace of mind.

"Chastity?"

"Sorry, Father. I was being rude." She looked up, surprised to see a wide smile on her father's face.

"That's all right, my dear. I'm sure it's just the pressure."

"Pressure?" *I'll say! The pressure of wanting—and damn near needing—a man who affects me like poison ivy.* What an itch he'd started! She'd gone to bed last night and sleep had been the furthermost thing from her mind. Instead she remembered the time in the maze, the images getting hotter as she relived the moments until finally she'd had no choice but to satisfy herself. Not that it had been complete satisfaction, but at least she'd relaxed enough so she could close her eyes. Chastity wondered if Sin had been forced to do the same. She hoped so. She refused to be the only one suffering.

Her father gave her a questioning look. "The pressure of the wedding. Brigit's your best friend. I know you want her precious day to be perfect."

"That's right. I do."

"I'm sure Sin wants that for his brother, too."

"I'm sure he does," she answered carefully, in response to the sly expression she could swear was lurking in her father's eyes.

"Together you must see that it happens."

"We should have peace and harmony between us, you mean?"

Reverend Goodwin smiled. "That's one way to put it, I suppose."

Chastity couldn't agree more. Unfortunately, peace and harmony was more the speed of her relationship with Jeremy. Her relationship with Sin was full of chaos and discord and hunger, which was—damn him—more exciting than she could have ever imagined.

"So you're seeing him this evening?"

"Who?"

"Really Chastity, I'm becoming concerned about you. Are you getting enough sleep?"

Blushing, she said, "Not exactly."

Reverend Goodwin's gaze sharpened until Chastity wanted to raise a shield. "I was referring to Sin, of course. Are you seeing him tonight?"

"Oh." For a moment she said nothing else, then pulled herself together to continue. "He visited the Renaissance Festival last night—"

"I heard," Chastity's father added with a dry expression.

What had he heard? And from whom? Chastity rushed on, "Sin had never been…so he ca-came." How close he came to coming she hoped her father would never find out. "Anyway he offered to take me to a game mall tonight, that's what he does professionally, you know...." She paused, positive she was making a mess of this explanation. If only her father wasn't watching her so closely. She lifted her chin. "I said I'd go." She had no idea why she was being so apologetic. She was an adult, for heaven's sake.

"Good idea."

"You think so?" His tone was benign, but Chastity could swear she'd heard something underneath.

"Certainly. There's more to life than the sixteenth century, Chastity."

"Well, really, Father, I know that."

He smiled. "Sometimes I wonder."

The silence lengthened until Chastity took the plunge, hoping her father could help give her some direction. "Is there something you're trying to tell me about my life? Or maybe about Jeremy?"

"No, my dear. Life is much more fun when you discover it for yourself. As for Jeremy... Well, you must discover the truth of that for yourself, too." With that he blew her a kiss and walked out of the room.

"Damn. I hate it when he gets enigmatic." Chastity clasped the waist of the male mannequin she'd been working on, then looked around at her other lords and ladies. "Obviously, Father feels you're no substitute for reality. What do you think?" The only answer she received was the soft *rat-tat-tat* from a woodpecker on a tree outside.

Chastity worked steadily, managing to put the finishing touches on two more wedding costumes. That left only hers and a few minor adaptations to Brigit's to finish before the wedding. Her father had already left when she went upstairs to dress. She stood before her closet. "What do you wear to a game palace?" She thought for a few moments before reaching for a pair of slacks. Hesitating, she put them back and removed one of her favorite summer dresses. It was too hot for slacks, or so she told herself.

She took her time getting ready, carefully rubbing rose-scented cream into her skin, applying subtle makeup and fixing her hair—drawing it up and back from her face in an old-fashioned topknot, allowing falling tendrils to surround her face and rest on her neck.

When she flicked her sundress over her head, the silk slip glided over her body, followed by the gauze cloud of the overdress. As everything settled into place Chastity glanced in the mirror. The ivory color of the dress, with its smattering of ivory embroidery, was so warm and creamy that it reminded her of fresh buttermilk. She moved to and fro, delighted as always at the way the dress caressed her limbs and whispered around her ankles. Chastity knew it wasn't practical for wearing on a motorcycle, but at least it was full enough that she'd be able to mount the bike. And beyond that, she didn't care.

She stood still as the light from the window illuminated her. She looked like a bride, or a sacrifice, Chastity wasn't sure which. Impulsively she reached for the fresh flowers that always graced her dressing table in summer. Removing a daisy, she snapped off the stem and stuck it in her hair. Then she mentally kicked herself. *Get a grip! You're going to play computer games, you idiot. This is not a life-altering event.* She inhaled, then let her breath out in a long, slow exhale, attempting to control her nervousness. The doorbell rang. Stomach still jumpy, Chastity took a last glance in the mirror and left the room.

She approached the door and pulled it open, saying, "I didn't hear your bike. Did you bring a car instead?"

"Of course I brought a car," said Jeremy. "I don't have a bike."

Stunned, Chastity stared at him, her mouth opening and closing like a stranded fish before she recovered enough to say, "Jeremy! How nice."

He leaned down to give her a kiss, which she instinctively avoided by turning her head so his lips fell on her cheek.

Jeremy drew back and looked at her. "Miss me?"

"I...I've been very busy, with the wedding and everything. I didn't realize you were—" She bit her lip.

"Gone?" he prompted. "Well, I wasn't gone very long."

After a moment Chastity said, "It's lovely to see you." In one way it was. Jeremy looked wholesome, as usual, and rather boring—but safe. One part of her yearned for safe and settled, terrified at the upheaval that awaited her if she continued on her present path. Of course the other part of her...

"I have news," Jeremy said with a self-important puff of his chest. "There was a message on my answering machine the other night. It was Professor Mendleshom."

"Who?"

"You remember my old professor from Harvard?"

"Oh, yes, yes, of course. You've mentioned him." She glanced around his shoulder looking for Sin. It would be just her luck for him to roar up here and find Jeremy. Or for Jeremy to find him. Not that there was anything wrong with that, for either one of them, she thought, but for some reason, she'd much rather it didn't happen.

"He's retiring and has recommended me for his position."

"What position?"

Jeremy gave her a strange look. "Head of the English

Literature Department. I have an interview with the dean tomorrow. According to Dr. Mendelshom, the dean will take his recommendation."

"That's good." Chastity thought she heard the faint throbbing of a motorcycle engine, so she rushed to finish the conversation. "Good luck. You deserve it."

"And there's a part-time position there, too, in Renaissance literature. You'd be working under me."

Surprised, Chastity pulled her attention from the noisy car that had just passed. "Under you?" She didn't like the sound of that. It smacked of the chauvinism that she'd so often encountered in institutions of higher learning.

Jeremy took her hands. "Don't you see what this could mean to us?"

Uneasy, Chastity attempted to smile. "Not exactly. It sounds wonderful for you, though."

"It's what we've talked about, Chastity. I guarantee this move will be much more beneficial than being a professor at our small college."

"I like our college. It has an excellent reputation."

"Of course it does. But it's not Ivy League. That's important to our research and publication future, you know." He squeezed her hands, smiling down at her. "Not to mention our personal one."

"Jeremy, I've been promoted to a full professor and awarded tenure. Why would I leave that to take a part-time position in your shadow?"

"I'm not suggesting you would be in my shadow, Chastity."

Chastity met his eyes, noting his sincerity as well as his impatience with her question. It wasn't his fault that he was more at home with books, scholarship and dusty academia than he was with people. It didn't make him a bad person, but he wasn't right for her. Funny that she should realize this now, on the porch waiting to meet another man. If for no other reason, Chastity thought, she'd always be grateful to Sin O'Connor for saving her from making a very big mistake with Jeremy. She might not have regretted that mistake right away, but she would have gotten narrower and narrower in focus until she'd shriveled up inside.

Gently, she withdrew her hands from his. "Jeremy. I know this isn't the time or the place, but—" A loud drone filled the air—the sound of a motorcycle driven at top speed. "You and I…"

"You and I?" Jeremy prompted.

"I value your friendship, Jeremy. I really do. However, I've been mistaken in some areas. I don't think we're suited for a personal relationship, after all. Something just doesn't feel right. I didn't realize it before, but now—" The angry sound of Sin's engine grew louder. Chastity caught a glimpse of him roaring down the street, as if he were anxious to reach her.

Jeremy looked first at Chastity, then turned to glance over his shoulder at the noisy machine. He snapped a glance back to her again, staring for a moment. As he studied her, his expression changed from expectation to disappointment and finally—as he threw another glance over his shoulder to Sin now parking at the curb—to disbelief. "I see."

Chastity wondered what Jeremy saw. Did he see the confused emotions pass over her face as she glimpsed Sin dismounting? Or the raw hunger she felt as Sin walked around his bike with that easy pantherlike grace of his? She was aware of Sin pausing by the gate, watching them.

Jeremy folded his arms and looked down at Chastity. "Well, well, well…this is a surprise."

"Jeremy, I'm so sorry. Even though we had no formal agreement, I know we'd fallen into the habit of—"

She gulped, the knowledge of her physical and emotional response to Sin fueling her resolve. "I feel it would be best if we considered ourselves exclusively friends and colleagues from now on."

Jeremy tucked his hands in his pockets, for a moment seeming less self-assured than Chastity had ever seen him. "I'm sure you're right."

Chastity smiled, trying to take the sting out of any emotion he might be feeling, not sure if it was actually emotion or pride. Either way, she never wanted to hurt him. "After all, you'll probably be off to Harvard where you'll be a huge success. I know I'll be reading brilliant papers and books from you before—"

Jeremy held up his hand. "No more than I'll read from you. You can be an outstanding scholar—the equal of your mother, I'm sure—if you give it your complete attention." For a moment more he looked at her, then glanced at Sin, now strolling slowly up the sidewalk, eyes glued to them. "Your company's getting impatient."

Chastity followed his glance. "Yes."

Sin reached the bottom of the stairs. Casually he lifted his leg to hook his heel on the step in front of him. "Hey, there."

Jeremy walked over and leaned down to shake hands. "Hello, yourself. Come to visit Chastity?"

"Uh-huh. And you too, I see."

The note of jealousy in Sin's voice thrilled Chastity, even as it appalled her. She wasn't a bone to be tugged between two dogs.

"I just stopped by to give Chastity some news about my potential job offer. One academic to another, you understand."

Sin nodded. "Oh, I understand absolutely. Academics—same minds, different bodies."

Chastity frowned. It was statements like that that

made her want to strangle the man. She exhaled with a small exasperated sound that elicited a grin from Sin.

Jeremy looked from him to Chastity. "Where are you two going?"

"We're going to play games."

Taken aback, Jeremy said to Sin, "What type of games?"

"Computer games."

"I didn't know you liked computer games, Chastity."

"I don't. I think they do nothing but corrupt the mind of today's youth and compromise the future by taking away imagination and replacing it with limited semireality."

Sin laughed. "Now, Doc, you promised not to prejudge."

"I'm not. I'm keeping an open mind."

Jeremy's lips twitched. "Yes, it sounded like it."

Sin stared at him for a moment, then nodded. "What about you, professor? Wanna come along and see if she's right?"

"No." Jeremy replied so fast that Chastity was almost insulted. "I have to get going. I just dropped by for a moment on the chance that I'd catch Chastity here. She usually is, if she's not at the college...or the festival."

"Not a partying sort of girl you mean?"

Chastity scowled. "What's that supposed to mean?"

Sin laughed. "Just getting some insight from someone who's known you a lot longer, that's all."

"If you want insight," Chastity snapped, "ask me. I'll be glad to give it to you."

"I've noticed."

"On that note," Jeremy said, "I'll leave you two to your games." He smiled at Chastity and descended the steps, stopping to shake Sin's hand. "Good luck." With great dignity he walked to his parked car, stopping abruptly to send them a brief wave before getting in and driving away.

Chastity watched Jeremy leave, suddenly scared by what she'd done. In one moment she'd broken or at least bent the hell out of a longtime relationship, and for what? For this devilish charmer standing in front of her? How stupid was that? Then she realized that no matter what she told herself, she hadn't really done it for him. Sin was part of it, of course, but she'd really done it for herself. For the her she was beginning to find inside. After a moment, she smiled, then descended the steps, stopping above Sin to look down into his eyes. "Are you ready for me to whip your butt at Pac-Man?"

A laugh exploded from Sin. "How far behind the times are you, anyway, Doc?"

Chastity rubbed her finger over her chin, "Oh, about four or five centuries, I guess."

Sin took her arm. "I'll say." He ushered her down the sidewalk to his bike and helped her mount the seat. "Watch that pretty dress. Tuck it up well so it doesn't get caught on anything."

Chastity lifted her skirt to her knees and managed to climb with semigrace onto the back of the motorcycle, taking care to gather the dress under and around her so it didn't blow over her head. "I haven't been to this game mall. Where is it exactly?"

He glanced over his shoulder. "I've changed my mind. We're not going there."

"We're not?"

"Nope. We're going to a better one. One where you can really experience everything technology has to offer all those dim-witted kids you described a few minutes ago." He started his bike, gunning the throttle.

She shouted over the noise. "Is this place far from here? I've never ridden on a motorcycle."

Sin ginned back at her, then pointed at the sky. "Not too far. We'll hang a left at the first star on the right." He lifted his heels and the bike began rolling forward. He reached to pull her arms around his waist. "Hold on tight, Doc. I don't want to lose you now. I'm about to introduce you to a whole new world."

As THEY TRAVELED through the early evening, Sin lied to himself, swearing that his determination to show her his own computer lab wasn't because of the way she felt nestled behind him on the bike. It wasn't because her arms hugging his waist felt like a band of wildfire, igniting related conflagrations all the way to his toes, or because her breasts felt so soft as they pressed against his back. Or because of the way her legs fit around his, the inside of her thighs cupping the outside of his as she nestled behind him on the bike. It wasn't even because he'd paced the floor most of the last night after he'd left her, either. No. He was taking her to his home because she didn't understand the power of the future and he was determined she would. That's all.

He turned his head against the wind, far enough so he could yell, "Comfortable?" over his shoulder.

"Yes... Oh, no!"

Sin started to slow down. "What's wrong?"

"My daisy fell out."

He laughed and sped up again. "We'll get you another one."

What a paradox this woman was. *Her daisy*. He'd noticed that daisy, perched up in that little mound of hair on top of her head, looking as comfortable as a crown. Some women were made for jewels, Sin thought, but Chastity Goodwin was made for daisies. She had that fresh, moist appeal that reminded him of wildflowers on a summer morning, the dew still kissing the petals as first light touched them. He wanted to see her that way, waking up to the world. With any luck, he would.

He turned off the main artery that crisscrossed the town of Gloriana onto a back road where he opened the throttle. The cycle leaped forward. "This is what it's all about."

Chastity's voice echoed faintly in his ear. "What is?"

Sin was going too fast to explain. But this was living—empty road ahead, a glorious setting sun, the promise of a starry evening sky above, and a sexy-as-hell woman straddling him. This was more than most men would ever ask for. But he wasn't most men.

9

SIN CONTINUED DOWN the road until he reached a small independent airfield far outside town. He turned, then angled to the right, driving onto a blacktopped lot. Braking to a stop, he steadied the bike.

Confused, Chastity murmured in his ear. "This is an airport."

Sending her a look, he said, "That's right."

"They have a game mall in this place? It's so small, where do they—?"

Sin dismounted, then helped Chastity do the same. "This is the only the first stop on your road to enlightenment."

Chastity wrinkled her nose, looking so adorable that Sin couldn't resist dropping a kiss on the tip of it. "Patience, Doc. We're going to take the bird the rest of the way."

"What bird?"

Sin jerked a thumb at a hangar sitting off to the left, with a silver helicopter parked in front of it.

"We have to take a helicopter? What's the matter with taking the bike? I rather like the bike."

Grinning, Sin said, "Do you? Then I'll have to take you for a ride again, won't I?"

A smile lit her eyes, making them only slightly warmer than her smiling lips. "I'd like that. There's something about riding through nature at that speed that's incredibly energizing."

He caressed her ear with his fingertip, noticing her

shiver when he touched her. "Are you telling me it turned you on, Doc?"

Chastity's cheeks turned pink as she glanced away from him. "I...only meant..." After a moment she looked him in the eyes and said truthfully, "Yes."

Gazing at her as she stood in front of him, slightly flushed and disheveled and more appealing than she had a right to be, Sin's gut twisted with desire. The emotion was so fierce and unexpected he wanted to pick her up and run away with her to somewhere no one would find them. Then he realized that's exactly what he was going to do. He grabbed her hand and pulled her toward the hangar, calling for the maintenance worker as he did so.

A middle-aged man in oily coveralls and a ball cap came running toward him. "Hey there, Billy," Sin said. "I'm taking her out again. Let's gas up and check 'er out."

"Yes, sir, Mr. O'Connor." The man got to work and within half an hour Sin and Chastity were seated inside and Sin was going over his pilot's checklist, making notations and tapping gauges.

Chastity fastened her seat belt, looking over to say, "How far are we going anyway?"

"About thirty minutes of flight time."

"Thirty minutes?"

Sin adjusted his headset, removing one from his ear to ask, "Does flying bother you? Is this a first experience like the motorcycle?" He'd thought he'd heard something odd in her tone. Maybe it was his imagination.

With a defensive lift of her chin, Chastity replied, "I hate to disappoint you, but I've flown many times—in aircraft held together by chicken wire it seemed—with my mother's expeditions. Plus, I've ridden into all types of strange and remote areas on the backs of donkeys and other four-legged beasts. I've also ridden in cars so rickety the junkyard wouldn't have them."

"Okay. Since you're such an experienced traveler, Doc, we're wasting time."

Chastity sent him a challenging look. "Not on my account."

Sin nodded, then flicked his switches, talked to the control area and lifted off. He banked to the left in a long slow turn designed to head northeast. "I love to fly. I fly everywhere."

"I thought you were into motorcycles."

"I am, but generally I ride a bike after I get where I'm going. If I'm going beyond my usual commute, I make arrangements to hire a bike, like I did here. Or I get a fast-as-hell car."

"What's your usual commute?" She waved at the luxurious interior of the chopper. "From all indications, you don't live in the suburbs."

Sin laughed. "Nope. I live in Vermont, in the mountains. My company offices are in Boston."

"You fly in every day?"

"No. Usually about two or three times a week, depending what's going on. I have very efficient people working for me. Sometimes I stay at my place in Boston, but generally I spend a lot of time at home in my lab."

"Your lab wouldn't be the game mall we're visiting would it?"

Sin grinned at the suspicious look on her face. "Now that you mention it..."

"I should have known."

"Settle back and enjoy the flight, Doc. There's something about flying at the beginning and the end of the day that gives you the chills." He indicated the round bubble of glass that seemed to bring the thick forests of Vermont so close they could touch them. "Take a look at the way the sun grabs at the trees 'cause it doesn't want go to bed. Each day it hangs on with everything it's got until the earth gets the better of it. You gotta admire it."

"That was worthy of a classical poet," Chastity said.

Sin could almost feel his face flush. *A poet? Maybe so.* He focused on the landscape in front of him. Poetry came from deep feelings and no matter how often he saw this sight from the air, it still moved him. He hadn't revealed it to anyone, though, not until now. They flew in silence for quite a while, but he could feel Chastity stealing glances at him, probably wondering what the hell he was up to. Well, he didn't know, exactly. He was playing all of it by ear...sort of like at the start of any new project. After a bit, Sin pointed straight ahead into the trees, correcting his position to prepare for their descent. "If you look up there you'll see a clearing. That's where we're landing."

Chastity nodded, leaning forward to watch the ground rush to meet them, the whirling blades flattening the grass and foliage as they settled down, perched on a small elevated clearing in the middle of the forest. "It's like being on top of the world," she said reverently.

"Nah, it's just in the middle of nowhere. At least it seems so when you approach it from the air. Actually there's a small town about ten miles away."

She looked around. "I don't see a house."

"We need to go that way a bit." Sin pointed to a road that led into the woods, but headed toward a set of buildings at the edge of the clearing. "We'll take the Jeep."

As Sin helped her out of the helicopter, Chastity said, "We're setting a record for transportation, aren't we? All we need is a camel or something and we've covered almost every possibility."

Sin laughed, opening the door of a blue four-by-four that had seen better days. "I'll see what I can do next time." He watched Chastity climb in before hopping in himself. Turning the key, he gunned the motor and took off down a winding road, steering casually around the twists and turns until the road straightened out.

"Oh, how beautiful," Chastity breathed as they topped a small ridge and she saw a lake and a house nestled in a hollow down below. "Look how clear the water is. And that house...it's breathtaking."

"I think so." Sin never tired of seeing it. The home was very modern in design, all stone, heavy timbers, gleaming glass and angles. The expanse of windows caught the reflection of the lake and the trees and brought them inside, seeming to absorb them. "I wanted a place that was modern in design, but still comfortable."

Awed, Chastity turned to him. "From the looks of it, you've succeeded."

"I'm glad you like it." How glad he was surprised him. Sin drove down the slight hill and around the lake to reach the driveway that circled the front of the house. Parking by the entrance, he helped Chastity from the car and escorted her up the cedar stairs that led to the deck that encircled the house. Unlocking the door, he pushed it open and waved her in, hoping she'd approve of the interior as much as she approved of the exterior.

FROM THE MOMENT Chastity stepped inside the double doors, from the instant her feet hit the chunks of flagstone that formed the foyer, she felt as if she'd come home. Surprisingly, it echoed the feeling she'd always received from her grandmother's house. From all of Sin's positioning on the future and the purity of technology, she'd expected to find the environment stark and sterile. What she discovered instead was warm and eclectic and very appealing. She turned to Sin, who was hanging his leather jacket on a hook near the door. "It's breathtaking."

It was.

She looked up at the architectural ceiling soaring above her for two stories to reach a peak, the height emphasized by heavy timbers in natural hues. A wood spiral staircase rose just off center of the foyer, with balconies and hallways leading off at right angles on two levels. The levels were a mixture of enclosed rooms and open loft areas that seemed to float, suspended in space, reminding Chastity of the tree house platforms surrounded by branches that she'd built as a child. "This is unusual, the way you've designed the space." She glanced at him, positive she was correct. "You did design this house, didn't you?"

Nodding, Sin smiled. "I don't like to feel closed in."

"Or trapped?" Not that Chastity hadn't already realized this from the nonconformist clues he'd given her since they'd first met. It was different to see him in his own environment, however, to see how he expanded to fit his space.

To her right, three angular steps descended into a sunken living room that ran the width of the house and was dominated by a huge fieldstone fireplace in the center. The enormous hearth was surrounded by leather couches set at right angles to each other. She walked to her left and discovered a dining room dominated by another huge fireplace with a far door into what surely would be the kitchen. Retracing her steps to the hallway, she peered straight ahead until she could see into what was obviously the entertainment room. She glimpsed part of a pool table, no computers, though. She peeped to the side to see Sin leaning against the railing that led upstairs. He looked at ease, a half smile on his face as he watched her.

As if he knew she was falling in love with this place.

Chastity wanted to explore everything, touch everything, absorb everything, from the books that lined the shelves to the flowers that tumbled over the self-standing planters on the deck outside. Her response to the ambiance of the house lowered her guard. She'd expected to use Sin's home to drive another wedge in the gulf between them. Instead she was amazed at how at ease she felt. That disturbed her.

Sin was watching her, much too closely, she thought. "Not what you expected, eh, Doc?"

"Different, certainly." She couldn't keep her voice cool any longer, "but absolutely marvellous. No wonder you like working at home." She turned in a semi-circle, staring at the soaring windows. "Doesn't it make you nervous at night, though? All that darkness and nothing between you and it but glass?"

He smiled and walked over to a box on the wall, flinging it open to flick a switch. Instantly, motorized vertical blinds that were cleverly hidden in the framework of the windows, marched out to cover the glass, enclosing the house, making it cozy. "This is for the times you want to shut everything out. Most of the time though, I leave them open. It's amazing…when you can see the stars and the moon shimmering on the lake, it gives you a new respect for how truly insignificant we are."

"First a poet, then a philosopher. What else are you Sinclair O'Connor?"

"A man in search of the future." He smiled. "A game player starting a quest."

"Okay," Chastity tilted her head, considering him, aware of the energy and emotion he usually kept leashed, remembering when he'd released it the night before. "Show me what I'm missing. That's why we're here, right?"

Sin nodded, then walked across the foyer to tuck her hand in his arm. Chastity started to walk forward, stopping to look at him as he directed her to the stairway instead. She pointed at the area off the end of the hallway. "Isn't that your game room back there?"

"That's one of them. But the one I want you to see is upstairs."

As Chastity followed him up the stairs, she said, "This isn't one of those 'let me show you my etchings' excuses to ravish me, is it?"

"Do I need an excuse? After last night and the night before," he whispered.

Chastity met Sin's eyes. His mischievous expression made her blush until she was positive the tip of her nose was glowing brighter than Rudolph's Christmas beacon. "Probably not," she muttered, knowing full well that he had only to raise an eyebrow and crook his finger and she'd fall into bed with him. Of course, she'd have to protest first, if she had enough breath left.

"Do *you* need an excuse, Doc?"

Stunned at his insight, she blurted, "Probably."

Sin caressed her chin and chuckled. "We'll have to see what we can do about that, won't we?"

At his words and his touch, especially when he ran this thumb over her bottom lip, Chastity shivered, trying to find a way to beg him to put his thoughts into action without seeming like a sex-starved spinster. She swallowed and looked up at him, knowing her eyes were probably showing him everything she was thinking, but trying to hide it anyway. "Where are you taking me?"

He leaned over and pressed a kiss on her lips. "Anywhere you want to go, darlin'. But right now, up to my lab."

Chastity tried to slow her breathing. "I always think of labs as being down in the basement...dungeonlike things."

"You must read a lot of strange stuff, Doc. Or else you've seen a lot of 1940 horror movies."

Chastity chuckled as she followed him up the stairs to the third level. "Come on, you have to admit when you say the word *lab* the first thing that comes to mind is Dr. Frankenstein."

Sin laughed as they emerged onto the third-floor balcony. He walked to the end of the hallway and opened a door, saying with a mock sinister accent, "Come into my la-bor-a-tory, Dr. Goodwin, and see the monster I've created for you."

Chastity stepped inside. Here was the sterile environment she'd thought to see from the beginning. At least it seemed so at first glance. The room was painted white and was full of computer workstations sitting on equally white surfaces. The computer faces were black holes, but the blinking green lights indicated the machines were merely at rest. "Why so many computers? Do other people work here with you?"

"Sometimes, but usually I use these computers for different applications and testing."

"Oh." Chastity continued to examine Sin's environment. Two alcoves on either side of the spacious room deviated from the rest of the area's layout. One alcove contained a chair, rather like a dentist's chair with a helmet and gloves situated to the side along with another computer. The other alcove contained a desk, bookshelves and all the traditional accoutrements of an office, including papers piled high, a wall-mounted bulletin board with work-in-progress notes and sketches pinned haphazardly to the surface. Chastity pulled her gaze from the messy desk and sent him a teasing glance. "Not as neat as I'd expect, Mr. O'Connor."

"As long as no one touches anything, I can find everything, Dr. Goodwin."

"Uh-huh," she said. For all of the white in the room and the efficiency of the layout, the lab didn't have the touch-me-not quality she'd expected. Perhaps that was because of the power of Sin's personality or perhaps it owed something to the painted mural at the far end of the room. It looked as if someone had just thrown colored paint at the wall and allowed it to splatter as it might into a rainbow of hues and intensities that challenged the eye and the senses. The more she stared at the abstract display, the more she became aware of the patterns hidden within the tone. Rather like the Magic Eye prints, those out-of-registration images that hid pictures within pictures within pictures. Chastity stepped forward. The closer she got the more the pictures changed. She saw planets, outer space, animals, primordial man…a cosmic mix of creation, both past and future.

"What do you think?" Sin asked, indicating the wall.

"It's very unexpected. Just when you think you see one thing, you see something else."

Sin joined her, standing shoulder to shoulder to stare at the painting. "A bit different from the classic art of your Renaissance period?"

"Yes," Chastity said slowly. "But no less powerful. What's your reaction?" She ached to know him better, this man so full of contradictions. She'd begun an acquaintanceship with his body, but now needed one with his mind as well.

"To me, it's the unknown quality of the future. Of the images we have yet to find and understand, of the worlds we have yet to conquer, from the inner world to the outer world. From sickness to science to entertainment." Sin walked over to touch the wall. "To me this mural is a microcosm of life."

"That's pretty heavy for a man who designs games, isn't it?" She saw his wince and rushed into an apology. "I'm so sorry. I didn't mean to sound insulting. I only meant, this isn't what I'd expect from someone who designed—" Confused, she stopped and spread her hands. "What games have you designed? Have I heard of any of them?"

Sin laughed. "You insulted one of them the first time we met."

"The one with the dreams and nightmares and that scary doctor?"

"One of my bestsellers."

"What's another one?"

"DragonStorm, Chained, Apocalypse. Any of those sound familiar? I do a lot of fantasy adventure games."

"The kind that hooks kids so they sit in front of these computers for days and don't do anything else but stare at a screen?" Chastity shook her head, making a distasteful face. "Lord, Sin, that drives people like me wild! I'd rather emphasize reading and learning to exercise the brain."

"Lighten up, Doc. Those games are fun, enjoyable, entertaining and they do teach things, like hand and eye coordination, mental skills like problem solving…"

"How about alienation? We're creating a nation of alienists, Sin. People who can't communicate unless their hands are on a keyboard. What about face-to-face conversation and connection? What's technology doing about that?"

"Chastity, technology has the answer to many of the world's problems."

She put her hands on her hips, leaning forward to

emphasize her point. "I think technology is creating many of the world's problems."

His fists hit his hips and his chin jutted out aggressively. "I've been working my butt off for fourteen hours a day for the past two years on technology designed to solve one of those problems. Come on…" He grabbed her hand and pulled her across the room to the alcove containing the chair. "Sit down."

"What is this? You're not going to pull my wisdom teeth are you?" She tried to make a joke because she found his intensity unnerving, even as she acknowledged she'd encouraged it.

"You're going to take a trip through my newest program." He picked up the gloves and fitted one then the other on her hands. "Okay, now the helmet."

"Why do I—"

"This is virtual reality. You're going to control the world and experience everything in it. Think of it as your Renaissance Festival in a computer."

Without another word he placed the helmet on her head. She now sat attached to a computer wearing technical accessories that made her feel like a refuge from a sci-fi flick. "This isn't going to be one of your nightmare worlds?"

"Why don't you see for yourself. There should be a door in front of you. Lift your hand and turn the knob."

Dreading the action, but too curious with the seeming reality of the picture that had appeared in front of her, Chastity obeyed. She turned the knob and stepped through into a scene that looked like a family picnic from the 1970s. She saw two little boys, one blond and one dark, a mom and a dad and an old barbecue grill. The mother was laughing as the boys romped with a golden-and-white collie that looked like Lassie from TV. She could feel the happiness in the scene, just as real as if she were there experiencing it. It was so real, Chastity thought. She could smell the scents of the hot dogs, taste the yellow mustard, hear the laughter. One of the children, the blond boy, ran to a swing hung from a tree and started to swing, while the dark-haired one chased the dog, not noticing how close he was moving to the swing. Then it happened, the swing arced forward. Chastity felt the fear and instinctively ducked, but too late. The swing hit the child, except it wasn't the child now. She could swear she was feeling the impact herself, a sharp blow to her forehead. The pain radiated outward and the world darkened for a long moment. Then she could feel arms around her and hear the comforting mother voice and see the panic in the blond boy's expression. The pain was still there, and the darkness—but so was the joy of being loved and cared for…it was so strong…so very real.

Confused, Chastity turned her head and immediately was in front of another door. The door to her house, she thought. *No, how can that be. Maybe it just looks like my house.* The door opened and she faced *herself*. She was standing in the doorway looking out at whom? The next moment Chastity entered the house, following herself into her workroom, now seeing herself surrounded by mannequins. Then she was on her knees in front of…Sin? She could swear she could feel his hands as they stroked up her body…smell the flowers on the desk, see the dust particles apparent in the shaft of light from the window. She heard birds, the clock ticking away the moments with a sharp click, then a…hiccup? Stunned, Chastity turned her head, searching for the real man. She turned so quickly that the scene changed and she felt as if she were falling…falling, scattering outward, her matter becoming part of the universe's. Until finally she stopped and coalesced into herself…yet not herself.

Chastity was lying on a carpet of flowers, wearing only a silk camisole and panties. The air was ripe and expectant, as if she were about to discover the mystery of life. Her skin was tingling, the tension rising until it rode lightly on the surface, ready to deepen. She sighed, the air slipping between her parted lips. As she rolled her head, she could see a man, the man whose hand skimmed over her flesh. She could see Sin. Pure Sin, as Eve must have seen it—beckoning, tempting, unable to resist. The hunger overwhelmed her, beginning at her toes and working its way up—

Then there was confusion. The feeling stopped and started, as if it were no longer real but imagination. The sharp edge of reality disappeared. Chastity ripped off her gloves and removed her helmet. She turned in her chair searching for Sin, who was standing next to the computer. She showered him with questions.

"What—what is this? Where did it come from? I don't understand. It was real, then not real. Why was I there? At the end I felt more like a voyeur than—"

"Than someone who re-experiences memories and events?"

"Yes."

"I told you technology was working to understand the world's problems?" Sin nodded at his computer. "That was an example of it."

"How? How can a bunch of random scenes and emotion…with me in the middle—" Chastity rubbed her forehead. "I don't understand."

Sin glanced away for a moment, before meeting her eyes. "I've been working on research to help epileptics and those with chronic pain problems," he said slowly. "The idea is to recreate the brain, the emotions, images, understanding, interpretation…to try to figure out how it works. How the brain selectively blocks some things and then works to reroute others."

"I thought you designed games?"

"I do." Shoving his hands in his pocket, Sin stepped away from the computer. "But maybe there's more to me than what you see, or think you see. There usually is to most people."

"How did you get involved with this?" He was right; there was more to him than she could have ever imagined.

"A childhood accident."

"The swing?" Remembering the image, she still felt his pain so vividly that she'd wanted to be the one to love and comfort him.

Sin nodded. "I had a number of lingering problems, all gone now, thank God. But for a long time..." He retreated into memories for a moment, before giving her his attention again. "Then there's this lady who works for me, a good friend, who has a child who is an epileptic. Sean's a great kid. I'd taken him to the ballpark one day to see the Red Sox play. He had a seizure, a bad one. After that I started looking into why the brain has seizures. What happens to the brainwaves?" Sin came forward, pulling his hands from his pockets, spreading them wide in his eagerness to explain. "My own curiosity...I couldn't let it rest. Then before you know it, I'm in touch with brain surgeons and psychologists, scientists doing research all over the world. So I recreated a brain in the computer."

"Using your brain, your thoughts, your images."

"Yes."

"In other words, I just walked through you. I saw and felt what you were seeing and feeling?" He looked away for a moment, seeming uncomfortable, but Chastity continued probing. "What you were wishing or dreaming about?" *Me. He's been dreaming about me.* The knowledge took Chastity's breath away. She wanted him more than she'd ever wanted anything in the world.

Sin met her gaze then, looking deeply into her eyes. "Yes."

"The field of flowers," Chastity whispered, "does it exist?" She hoped so. When she'd seen herself reaching up to him...reaching for the man poised above her, and seen the longing in her face, she realized just how important he'd become to her. How much she wanted to give to him, just as she felt his yearning to give back to her. He filled her world. Chastity had the strangest feeling that it was more than just sex...for both of them. She gripped Sin's arm. "Does it?"

"Yes," Sin whispered.

"Then take me there. I want that experience to be real, too."

"Chastity." He groaned her name.

"Now. Take me there now. I can't wait any longer. Let's see if we can make history repeat itself." She was amazed at how she was shedding her inhibitions layer by layer.

Grasping her hands he pulled her from the chair into his arms. "Some of those images were the future, not history, darlin'."

Chastity drew his head down to hers, whispering against his lips. "It'll be history soon enough." Their lips touched in a hot, lingering kiss. A kiss that had been building since he'd picked her up earlier.

Suddenly, Sin released her and moved like a whirlwind, ushering her to the door and down the steps so rapidly that Chastity felt dizzy. Or perhaps she was already dizzy and his action accentuated it. He hustled her down the hallway, stopping only to remove a blanket from a carved chest before he reached the back door of the kitchen and they stepped into the warm summer night of the garden beyond.

Chastity looked up. The moon had risen, a full moon that illuminated the earth below with a subtle light and turned the trees into paper cutouts in a children's book. Chastity opened herself up to feeling. She stared at the man leading her through the night so confidently. Sin, she thought, the wonder of him filling her mind. This man unleashed something wild and free inside her. Something she'd never felt before. She smiled to herself, realizing that Sin had somehow managed to do what no one else had done, or ever attempted. He'd unchained all her inner desires, desires she hadn't even realized she had. Watching his firm buttocks and long legs eat up the path, Chastity hungered to release the rest of them.

She didn't have long to wait.

They emerged from the trees into a small clearing, a space sprinkled with black-eyed Susans, Queen Anne's lace and lavender, dappled by moonlight, highlighted by fireflies and filled with the dizzying scents of summer.

"How beautiful," Chastity said.

"Fit for a queen, your majesty," Sin said with a smile, taking her hand and continuing to walk. When he reached the center of the clearing, he removed the blanket he'd tossed over his shoulder and spread it on the ground, trying to keep from crushing the flowers as he did so. Hands trembling a bit—from excitement or fear, Chastity wondered—he bent to smooth the edges of the woven cotton. He paused, staring down at the cloth, then turned to look at her, reached to touch her. He smoothed his palms up her arms. "Does your skin still taste like sweet cream?"

Chastity hesitated, her lashes sweeping down to cover her eyes. After a moment she met his gaze. "Why don't you find out."

Needing no further urging, Sin skimmed his hands

over her shoulders, his fingertips dipping down to
trace the neckline of her dress, before his lips followed
their path. He pressed small kisses across the tops of
her breasts, impatiently moving the fabric aside to reveal more of her, then dropped to his knees on the
blanket. He moved his mouth over her, starting the descent into pure pleasure. Chastity could feel the heat of
his lips through the light silk of her dress as he pressed
kisses on her rib cage, at the curve of her waist, de-
scending to her stomach, his mouth and hands moving
lower as he sat back on his heels. His hands swept over
her from hip to ankle, then slipped beneath the flowing
fabric to travel upward again. He raised his head and
looked at her. "I think you're wearing too many
clothes."

She slipped her fingertips into his hair, smoothing it
back from his face. "I think we're both wearing too
many clothes." She stretched in a sinuous catlike move
that thrust her pelvis toward him, moaning a little as
he nipped her, as the heat flooded her. "I want you to
ravish me." Chastity wanted him to throw her to the
ground and take her. She didn't want gentleness, only
aggressive urgency would satisfy her at the moment.

She should have known Sin would do no such thing.
He never did as she expected. Instead he lay back on
the blanket like the main course in an orgy. He smiled,
a ripe sexy tilt of his lips that made her ache to savor
them. Like a man who had all the time in the world, he
studied her. Each place his eyes touched burst into
flame, heating her until the dress she wore was an almost unbearable encumbrance. Chastity felt she'd go
mad. Then he said, "Touch me."

She needed no more urging, pleased to play the ag-
gressor—a role she'd not been accustomed to in relationships. A role she felt destined to play tonight.

Leaning down, bending over him until her neckline

gaped, she ran her hands over the muscles in his chest, delineated by the simple white shirt. She marveled at the way the cotton molded itself to his contours, rising and dipping with the toned body underneath. Impatiently she pulled his T-shirt from his jeans, inhaling fiercely as she glimpsed his tanned flesh. Seeking more contact, she pushed the shirt up with a violent gesture that surprised a chuckle from him. "Ooh, did I scratch you? Sorry, I—"

Sin gentled her saying, "Easy, darlin', easy now. It's okay, don't stop."

His voice soothed her innate reserve as much as his body aroused her inner desires. She wasn't responding just to his sex appeal, but to the man she'd been introduced to moments before in the lab. The humanitarian. The man who had much in common with her father, with his desire to explore personalities, to help people reach deep into themselves and better realize their potential. She let down all her walls to respond to the man who'd been drawing her closer and closer since the moment they met. Since that moment in the doorway, that he'd recreated so vividly in his computer program.

Sin sat up, which moved him closer to her as he pulled the shirt over his head. His economy of movement might have fooled Chastity into thinking he was unaffected by her if she hadn't seen the fierce glare of desire in his eyes and the tension in his muscles. He lay back, proof of his arousal visible as he toyed with the snap on his jeans. Chastity slapped away his fingers, teasing, "Oh, no, you don't. My privilege."

He flung his arms out to the side. "Be my guest."

She pulled at the fastening, then reached for his zipper. Resting her fingertips on the metal teeth, she traced the zipper from top to bottom, bottom to top before meeting his eyes, which were now blazing gold.

Chastity gave him a fierce smile. "This is the way I want you." Grasping the zipper head she pulled, watching it slide down inch by inch to reveal an arrow of dark hair that pointed the way south to the top of his very brief black underwear. She slipped her finger under the elastic, saying with a saucy look, "I'm surprised you even bother to wear any."

Sin winked. "Have to or I'd get caught in my zipper, then I wouldn't be much good to you."

Chastity giggled, then sobered, her anticipation growing. "We wouldn't want that. 'Cause I want you to be very good to me." She rubbed her fingertip against his skin, watching as he inhaled sharply. Teasing, she started to withdraw, but he took her hand, thrusting it under his briefs.

"Don't stop, darlin'."

"Don't worry," she breathed, using both hands to yank his jeans and briefs down. He lifted his hips to help her. She pushed the clothing down his legs until they pooled at his ankles, with him helping her by slipping his shoes off, then pushing and kicking his pants off the rest of the way.

Chastity sat back on her heels and took her first real look at him. Lying there like a reclining Greek god, she could only think his body should be the subject of a study, too, not just his mind. He was gorgeous. Long, lean lines of muscle and tanned skin stood out against the ivory blanket like a sculpture struggling to reveal itself from marble. Only most sculptures didn't feature such impressive erections. And he *was* impressive, and was becoming more so by the minute. He rose full and firm from a thatch of black hair that invited her fingertips, but she didn't indulge herself—not yet.

"Touch me," he repeated.

She licked her lips. "Oh, I will. I most certainly will." With a wildness she'd never felt before, Chastity touched him with hands, then lips and tongue. She started at his toes, massaging and caressing them, before moving up to his feet, exploring the instep, the ankle, then up his calf to his thigh, thrilling to every murmur, every uncontrolled movement he made. Her fingertips skimmed over his hard muscle as she moved nearer to the core of him. He tensed as her fingertips slipped from the outside of his thigh to the inside. Her excitement building, Chastity tugged her dress to her knees so she could straddle him. Her fingers reached him, tangling in the nest of hair at the base of his penis. He jerked as she circled him, groaning as her fingers met to ring him, moving up from the bottom to the top.

"I love the feel of you," she said.

Unable to control herself, she leaned forward and ran her tongue over his velvety tip, smiling as he quivered in response. "The taste of you." She sucked him into her mouth. As she tasted him, she realized she'd never wanted to do this before, not with any other man. Not that there had been that many, but even so, she always found the thought remarkably unappealing. With Sin, she couldn't help herself. He made her feel feminine, desirable and made her realize she could release the animal in her without fear. At that thought, she sucked him deeper into her mouth, running her tongue over him, sucking harder as his hips rose instinctively. Her hands ran over his hips and chest, and her heart raced as she gave him pleasure, listening to his groans as he slipped his hands into her hair to hold her mouth steady on him.

She burned, her hot center wanting…needing contact with his. She writhed against his thighs as she enjoyed him, rubbing against him as her tension rose, so overwhelmed by the feel of him beneath her fingers and lips that she slipped from mere desire into sheer abandonment. Chastity looked at Sin, his face flushed with desire, mouth tight with passion, eyes probing the depth of her soul. And that's when she realized the devil had won.

I love him. Damn the man. I love him.

Thoughts raced through her mind. How could she tell him? Did she dare? What if this was merely desire, not real love? Perhaps she wasn't experienced enough to tell the difference.

"Hold on, darlin'," Sin gasped. "No more. I'm gonna explode."

Sin tore himself away from her. With a hot grunt, he grasped Chastity under the arms, pulling her up until she lay fully on him, as his body pulsated, his need to release still unsatisfied. His hands cupped her buttocks, pushing her against him, her thin frock the only thing between them. The dress was so silky it might as well not be there as far as he was concerned.

It won't be there long, Sin thought as he grasped the hem of her dress, which had now ridden up her thighs, and tugged it over her head. The overdress and the silky slip came off as one piece, revealing a skimpy silk-and-lace camisole. He cupped her breasts, rubbing his thumbs over the hard nipples poking up beneath the silk.

"You're just as I remembered," Sin said. Just as he'd been seeing her in his dreams every night since they'd met.

"When?"

Sin undid the flimsy ribbons that closed the camisole from the top to the waist. "When?" *Always, it seems.* "When I flew up here earlier today to do some work." The laces gave and her breasts spilled into his hands. "But all I could think about was you. I want you." He'd sat in his lab trying to concentrate, but she was there before him—wanting, needing…

Chastity thrust herself toward him, moaning urgently when his mouth closed over her sensitive nipples. "Have me. For heaven's sake, have me."

Sin rolled his tongue around the nub, then switched to the other breast, before pulling her forward to bury his face between them. Her hips ground against his in a movement as elemental as nature, as old as time.

Frantic now, Sin pushed the camisole off her shoulders, leaving her to ride him bare-breasted, hair falling down upon her shoulders like an Amazon queen. She rocked forward, wearing a strip of silk so brief, he had only to use one finger to slip it aside so he could enter her. He forced himself not to do so yet. He wanted her hotter—so hot she'd never remember anything but this. This moment in time and him—only him. He slipped one hand between their thrusting bodies and fingered her, wanting to die when he felt her slick heat. He was determined she'd be as frantic as he. As his fingers rubbed her, searching for the most sensitive part of her, he realized she was close. One finger found her, circling the nub until she jerked spasmodically.

"Please...oh please, Sin."

She tried to tear his fingers away, but they advanced instead, slipping into her, increasing in speed until she screamed. Sin ripped off her bikinis and urged her over until she lay facedown on the blanket. He mounted her from behind, one hand on her breast, one hand slipping around the front of her hips. His fingertips continued circling while his penis slipped between her legs to rub against her hot wet mound. Still in the midst of ecstatic foreplay, he didn't enter her, knowing that the minute he did it would be all over for him. Sin wanted to enjoy it as long as possible. He pressed small kisses on her shoulders, licking at the nape of her neck, biting her earlobe.

"Sin!" Chastity's legs tightened on him, forcing his

flesh against her wetness as she came, jerking frantically against his hand.

Sin couldn't take anymore.

He flipped her over on her back and poised himself over her. She reached for him—greedy for more—spreading her legs wide. "Again," she whispered, fiercely. "Again."

"Oh, baby," he murmured, stroking her from breast to hip. "I've never wanted anyone the way I want you." The minute he said it, he realized how true it was. The thought scared him, but he couldn't stop now.

Her lips pursed, their ripeness beckoning him to taste them. When she could breathe again, Chastity said, "Then take me, damn it. Take me."

Sin poised himself over her and slipped inside, trying to keep enough control of himself so he wouldn't ravish her. Which was what he felt like doing. He wanted to bury himself until he couldn't tell where he ended and she began. He pushed forward, inch by tiny inch. "No, don't close your eyes. I want to see you. I want to know how you feel when I get inside." He advanced at a steady clip, saying, "I want to watch you slip over the edge again."

She rocked forward, wrapping her legs around him until he was buried in her. Surrounded by her soft, wet heat, he started to move—slowly at first, then as he knew it would, his desire got the better of him. He thrust faster and harder, climbing higher and hotter, with Chastity keeping pace every step of the way. Until finally, they hit the gasping, groaning, screaming peak.

It was hard to come back to earth.

Eventually Sin, pulse still racing out of control, lifted his head and met Chastity's eyes. "Still alive," he panted.

"Barely," she whispered back, still gasping.

"That was incredible. I don't think I can move." Sin needed to make light of the situation. It had the potential of being much too important and that made him very uncomfortable.

With a smile, Chastity said, "I'm not sure I can walk."

"Me, either." Sin listened to the crickets' songs as the fireflies lit up the meadow. Something happened here that he wasn't prepared to deal with. He tried to think of what to say when—

"Sin…um…there's a weed poking me in the rear."

"I'm sorry."

Chastity coughed. "Uh…could you…" She coughed again.

"Oh! Yeah, I'll get off." *Get off?* Like he'd just hopped a bus? Stunned at his comment, Sin stayed put for a few seconds. He couldn't remember ever feeling this awkward with a woman, especially one with whom he'd just had mind-altering, blood-busting, hotter-than-hell sex.

Coughing again, Chastity gasped, "I can't breathe. You're heavy."

"Damn," Sin rolled off her like a rock going downhill. "Right. I'm sorry…guess I was squishing you, huh?" Sin lay facedown, not wanting to move any farther away—Chastity was too soft, too exciting, too comfortable…too *necessary*. Panic set in at the thought. *Wait a minute. Necessary? No. No woman is necessary to my life.* He flipped over onto his back.

They lay there in silence for a moment—the silence increasing the awkwardness. Sin was aware of Chastity stealing tiny glances at him, but all of a sudden he didn't know what to say. After all, he'd taken this woman, this woman so outside his usual experience, and practically worn a rut in the grass. At least the first time he'd been more gentle. At the moment, casual conversation wasn't easy. He sneaked a look. Chastity lay still, like an offering to the moon goddess. She met his gaze and Sin jerked his away, feeling like a small boy watching a forbidden video. He could feel the tension building again. Not the tension that had taken them to the brink of madness and beyond, but the "Oh my God what did I do, was I out of my mind because I scarcely know this person and I don't know what to do now!" kind.

How weird, Sin thought. *Maybe I've never cared enough to feel this uncomfortable.* He rushed to speak. "Great moon, huh."

"Yes." Reaching for the edge of the blanket to cover her nudity, Chastity said, "A full moon brings out the madness in people, or at least people used to believe that."

It still did, Sin thought as he watched her pull the blanket up to her chin. He wanted to strip it off her. *Think of something else.* Staring at the sky, Sin murmured "Star light, star bright, first star I see tonight I..." *God, I didn't use a condom—either time. What if...*

Chastity joined in, "I wish I may, I wish I might..." Her voice trailed off as she turned her head away from him.

He wanted to ask what she was wishing for, but he was terrified she'd answer. Just as he was terrified he'd open his mouth and tell her he was wishing for her— only her. It wouldn't work, him and her, Sin thought. He couldn't be tied down. He had work to finish. Important work. People were depending on him, he couldn't lose his focus, which is what would happen if she were around permanently. Good as this was, it was temporary. He knew it. She knew it. She'd be the first to tell him so if he mentioned it. After all, she had a career that mattered, too.

Chastity folded her hands over the blanket that scarcely covered her. The air felt as if a heavy cloud had descended on them. She didn't know what to say, how to bring back the connection she'd felt earlier, how to make contact with the man's mind now that she'd given him her body. She couldn't ask Sin. Then she noticed her clothing scattered around. *Maybe I should get dressed.* But she was suddenly nervous about sitting up and... Deciding to delay the movement, she stared up at the cool blue light in the sky, focusing on one twinkling pinprick of light.

"Do you think wishes ever come true?"

Because if they do, I'll wish for Sin in my life, no more Goody Two-shoes professor for me. Not that she'd been one a few minutes ago. Chastity almost groaned to think how aggressive she'd been. She swallowed a hiccup, pretending to cough instead.

"I dunno," Sin said, his voice sounding funny. "What do you think?"

Chastity really wanted to tell him, but couldn't. Her mind and mouth seemed frozen. *Keep it simple. Keep it simple. Whether I think I love him or not, this isn't for real. What happened here was so overwhelming and out of the ordinary that...* Completely confused, Chastity peeped at him from under her lashes, before she finally spoke. "I think you should always wish for the most urgent thing."

"Okay." He met her gaze then pulled his away. "Urgent. Let's see, um...maybe...okay, I got it. A few more hours of good solid work tonight."

Stunned, Chastity stared at him. "Work?" She'd just had the most intense experience of her life and he was thinking about work? Granted, his work was urgent and unbelievably important, but what about her? She wanted to scream—but she wouldn't, of course. She'd already appalled herself by stepping outside her personality tonight. Chastity covered her mouth but a small hiccup escaped anyway.

Sin sat up and reached for his pants, seeming not to have heard her nervous response. "Yeah. I'm getting close to a breakthrough. If I don't have any more distractions and keep at it—"

"Distractions! Is that what you call this? A distraction?" Obviously he couldn't wait to get rid of her.

"I didn't mean it like that." Sin tried to change the subject. "You might not realize how important it is that I finish what I'm doing, but I've got this dream…"

Chastity sat up too, gathering her clothes, trying to feel some anger so her hurt would take a back seat. "You're not the only one with dreams, Sin. You're just the one with the egotistical approach to them." After all she had a career, too. One that she'd spent her life preparing for.

"Egotistical?"

She donned her underclothes, then pulled the slip over her head. "That's right. All along you've assumed that what you believe is best—" She fought her way free of her dress, yanking it down. She had to get away from here before she threw herself at him again. Stupid, stupid. Obviously she was nothing but a fling. She should have known. With a man like this, what else could she be?

Sin sent her an astonished look. "Me? What about you?"

Chastity paused. "Excuse me?"

"You've been preaching at me since you met me, Doc. About the virtues of history, the value of the past."

"You're right. I have." She jerked her thumb, pointing to herself. "It's *my* dream to write a book that eventually shares that excitement of history with others.

Not in a college classroom like I do now, but with children long before they get there.''

Staring at her, Sin pushed his hair back. "Chastity, I…''

She stood up. "It's late. I need to go home." She didn't want him to talk anymore because she might throw herself at him and open her heart. This way at least she could keep her pride. Besides, she had to think of herself. She'd had a fulfilling and fascinating life before she met Sin. She still did.

"Home? I thought maybe you could…''

"Home," she said in a firm tone, her mouth drawn tight. "Back to where I belong." *Back to my tidy existence. Back to things I know. I don't want that to change. Do I?*

Sin reached for her, but she evaded him. "Chastity, what happened before—''

"Is history." Chastity folded her arms, hugging herself tightly. "In the past…dead and buried.''

Sin was silent for a moment. Finally he said, "Game over, you mean?''

"Game over," Chastity replied, making a huge effort to keep her tone level and quiet. How could it be anything else. He lived his life here, she her life there—both of them cozily ensconced in their own worlds. She slid a glance under her lashes, taking in the wildly mussed dark hair, the exciting lines of his face, the tempting curve of his lips, his taut body. A deep weariness swept over her.

The devil of it was that they'd met at all.

10

"CHASTITY. CHASTITY?"

Chastity turned away from her worktable. "What?" As much as she tried to concentrate, her mind kept straying to Sin.

Brigit placed one hand on her hip and stared at her friend. "Can I take my wedding dress off? Or do you still need to do something else?"

Chastity fumbled with the white pearl bands she held in her hand. "I...think..." She stared down at the pearls, the color as creamy as the blanket she'd lain on the night before. How could something that had been so right, end so wrong?

"Think?" Brigit prompted, beginning to tap her foot.

Chastity felt her eyes tear. She looked at the floor, blinking frantically to prevent them from falling. "I think...I should put more pearls around the neckline. Yes. Yes. I should..."

"Any more pearls and I'll look like an oyster." Brigit bustled across the room, as fast as her long gown would let her. "All right. What's going on? Is it Sin?"

Shocked, Chastity looked up. Brigit's concerned face wavered in front of her. Like a little kid, Chastity used the sleeve of her shirt to wipe away a tear. "What makes you think that?"

"Because you have the same look on your face that I had when Harrison told me there was no way we'd ever get married." Brigit rolled her head in exasperation. "Genetics being what they are, I figure his brother isn't much brighter."

Chastity's lips lifted into what would have been a smile, if there weren't so much misery behind it. At least she could still pretend she had a sense of humor. "He didn't mention marriage."

"Do they ever?" Brigit laughed. "Hell, Chastity, if we left it up to men, mankind would never survive."

Brigit's comment prompted a real smile from Chastity. "Good thing women came along, huh?"

"The best thing. We're the voice of reason. Women listen instead of flying into aggressive action, then we work to heal the problem." Brigit examined her nails for a moment, then examined her friend. "So, what's the trouble. What happened? Last time I saw you and Sin together, the air was so steamy I started to sweat in sympathy."

"It got steamier."

"Impossible." Brigit grinned and clapped her hands. "Tell, tell."

"Last night, he took me to his home in Vermont. Flew me there. Do you believe that?"

Brigit nodded. "Harrison mentioned Sin's chopper when I offered to pick him up at an airport, so I know he generally flies himself. So, what's his house like?"

"It's the most unbelievable place. I walked in and never wanted to leave, I felt so at home. It just felt right, do you know what I mean?" Chastity thought for a moment. She didn't know if it was really the home or the person who'd been with her.

"Come on...then what?"

"Then Sin took me to his lab and showed me his work. The work that's been consuming him."

"He's designing a new game?"

"No." Chastity waved her hand. "It's difficult to explain, but it has to do with computers and brain re-

search. But when he played the program and I saw…"
She shrugged, unable to put her feelings into words.

"Hmm… Harrison's never mentioned this aspect of
Sin's work."

"I think this research means so much to Sin that—"
Chastity stopped as she finally realized what he'd revealed her. She hadn't realized the significance before.
Sin had taken her to his home and shared the real man
with her. *The real man.* She'd seen, felt, touched, tasted
and lived inside the real man.

"Is he a good lover?"

Chastity blinked like an owl. "How did you
know—"

"Oh, please. It's written all over you."

"Oh, yes," she said, remembering the feel of him
against her. The heart-stopping heat of him.

"So, what's the problem?"

"Afterward, he…it was so…I didn't know what to
say. I was embarrassed and Sin was strange." Chastity
tried to analyze it, but it was still too fresh. "Then we
had this argument, sort of. He called me a distraction."

"Oh, that's good. That's very good." Brigit gathered
up her dress and plunked herself on the worktable.
"Harrison called me a distraction."

"Then Sin became so cold and distant. As if once
he'd had me, that was it. He scarcely said a word to me
at the wedding rehearsal this afternoon. Not that I said
anything to him, either, but still…"

"Are you sure Sin wasn't nursing his hurt?"

"Why should he be hurt?" Chastity huffed and
puffed. "I'm the one who got hurt." Did she ever.
She'd ventured out of her safety zone and discovered
how big and bad the world could be. Chastity wondered if the historical figures she loved had found their
world the same? Hadn't it been just as uncertain and
perplexing? For the first time Chastity suspected that

perhaps the only difference between the past and the future was perspective.

Brigit raised her hands, obviously trying to reassure her. "Perhaps *hurt* is the wrong word. Maybe I mean *confusion*."

Chastity made a face. "I'm the one who's confused, Brigit. One minute I'm in the arms of the man I'm in love with—" *Oh no!* Now Brigit would never leave this alone. And Chastity wasn't sure she loved him anyway...maybe it was just sex. Even though she knew it wasn't. This was the man for her. She just didn't know what to do about it.

"You are? Ooohh-eee, I knew it!" Lifting her dress awkwardly, Brigit leaped off the table and bounced up to Chastity. She threw her arms around her waist and squeezed. "Isn't this great? We'll be sisters."

Unwinding Brigit's arms, Chastity stepped away and started to pace. "We won't be any such thing. Haven't you been listening? He blew me off. Adios, *hasta la vista*, see you around, and 'buh-bye now!'"

"So what! You're not going to let a little thing like that stop you, are you?"

Amazed, Charity stared at her best friend. "A little thing? That's what you call a little thing?"

"Well, of course it is to a determined and smart woman. That's what you are, isn't it?"

Chastity thought about that for a moment as she recognized the sly look Brigit sent, the one her friend always used when she tried to talk Chastity into doing something generally idiotic. The funny thing was, if Brigit had asked her those questions a few days ago, Chastity would have agreed without hesitation. At the moment, however, she wanted to curl up and pretend the world had forgotten her.

Like an irritated bantam rooster, Brigit thrust her

chin forward, saying, "Chastity, I'm ashamed of you. Where's that old fighting spirit?"

"What fighting spirit? I've never been a fighter."

"Not overtly, maybe. But you're the subtle kind. The type that just hangs in there and eventually wears down the opposition."

Astonished, Chastity turned to look at her friend. "Why do you think that?"

Gesturing wildly, Brigit said, "Look at your child-hood…in and out of school, camping in jungles, name it. You might have been uncomfortable there and when you came back to school, but you never gave up. Instead you hunkered down each time and tried to do what was expected of you." Brigit sent her an admiring look. "That took guts, Chastity. It would have been easier to rebel, or be totally obnoxious or such a mouse that no one noticed you."

Chastity stroked her cheek with a thoughtful finger. "I never thought of it that way. I always keep comparing my achievements with other people's and thinking I don't measure up."

At that, Brigit shook her head. "You're so dense sometimes. The funny thing is, according to Harrison, Sin is exactly the same way. That's why Sin works so hard, why he's so driven. He was always trying to outdo his brother, while you were trying to beat your mother."

Chastity chewed that over for a moment. Of course she was always trying to outsucceed her mother, but that wasn't as bad as Brigit made it sound. That was what you were supposed to do, wasn't it? But Sin? Was that one of the keys to his personality, too? If so, how could she approach him? Did she even want to approach him? Confused, Chastity looked up.

"Brigit, I don't know what to do. On one hand I think I should rush over to the castle and either tie the guy to the bed until he listens or just kiss him until his eyes cross from staring at my nose close-up."

"Why don't you tie him up first, then kiss him senseless."

Chastity chuckled. "Actually that sounds pretty good."

"I agree." Brigit said, with a grin. "I might have to try it on Harrison tonight."

"This is your last night of freedom. How's it feel?"

"Heavenly—and terrifying." Brigit wagged her finger under Chastity's nose. "And if I hadn't swallowed my pride, I wouldn't be having it."

"What do you mean?"

"Harrison did something so stupid, so idiotic, so...so malelike before we left Paris that I never wanted anything to do with him again. I told him so, too. Then he told me back." Brigit thrust her hand through her hair, sending the pixie points up like the prickles of a hedgehog. "I was on my way to the plane, when I realized I didn't want to leave him, and I sure as hell wasn't going to let him leave *me*, even if he was a pigheaded idiot."

"What did you do?"

"I told the cabbie to turn around and went to tell him so."

"And you're suggesting I—"

"No. That's what *I* did." Brigit walked over to Chastity and hugged her. "The point I'm making is, I think you should do what is right for you."

"How do you know what that is? I mean, every time I think I know, I find another reason why I don't."

Brigit patted her dress and grinned. "When the time's right, you'll know."

Sending her best friend a suspicious look, Chastity said, "You're not going to say 'trust me' now, are you? 'Cause the last time you said—"

"No." Brigit's face grew serious. "Don't trust me, trust yourself."

SIN SQUATTED under a tree just inside the forest that surrounded Brigit's castle and wondered if he'd been born with one foot in his mouth, or whether sticking it in there sideways was something he'd learned later. He could still see Chastity's face as he remembered the gist of her conversation the night before. If he'd only kept his mouth shut, he wouldn't be sitting here with everything aching, from his heart to his hard-on, at the thought of Chastity. When he'd seen her earlier that afternoon at the wedding rehearsal, it was all he could do not to gallantly throw himself at her feet and let her step on him—on *him*—like Sir Walter-freakin'-Raleigh, but without the cape and the mud puddle.

"Sin, what the hell are you doing?"

Sin batted at the heavy foliage that surrounded him. "Harry." He peered out at his brother.

Harrison snorted with disgust as he parted a few leaves to better see Sin. "You look like an overgrown elf on the run, hiding out in the forest. What's going on?"

Sin stood up and brushed off his jeans. "Why do you think something's going on?" It wasn't that obvious that his heart was in shreds, was it?

"Oh, probably because you haven't said a damn word to me beyond a grunt since I saw you this morning."

"I could have things on my mind, you know." Like a corkscrew-haired redhead with a messed-up mind and a body that'd damn near killed him!

"Like what?"

"Stuff. Business stuff, new ideas..." Sin's only new idea at the moment involved covering Chastity with whipped cream then licking it off. Fat chance he'd ever have of making that come true now.

Harrison tried to keep his grin from showing, but didn't quite manage it. "Yeah, you could. But I wouldn't bet on it."

"Why not?"

"'Cause you look too miserable. It's gotta be a woman."

"I'm not miserable. I'm fine. I haven't met the woman who can make me miserable. I'm so fine I'm—"

Harrison propped his shoulder against a nearby tree. "Yep. Protesting too much. Definitely a woman."

"You're nuts." Sin's hands clenched into fists. "An' if you stand there looking like that much longer, I'll take you out so fast—"

"You and who else?"

Sin squared his jaw and stepped forward. Knowing his brother could never resist provocation he said, "You're asking for it."

"Go soak your head. You're not gonna pick a fight with me, when you'd rather fight with Chastity." Harrison thumped Sin in the chest with a pointed finger for emphasis. "'Cause if you fight with Chastity, then you can make up with Chastity. Get my drift? I think making up with Chastity would be a good thing for you."

"What makes you think I need to make up with her?" Would he even get a chance to try? Damn, he'd better. He didn't want to stay this miserable for the rest of his life.

"'Cause if your chin gets any lower to the ground, you'll have to roll it up in your pant leg."

Sin chuckled—he couldn't help it—then he sobered. "I called her a distraction."

Shaking his head, Harrison groaned. "Oh man, bad

move. Unless you told her you can't live without distractions?"

"No. It happened kinda fast, but I think she took it as if she were taking me away from more important things that I should be doing."

Harrison whistled, shaking his head. "That was really, really dumb."

Sin scowled. "Well, she is a distraction."

"Of course she is. All women are." Harrison punched Sin in the arm. "But you want 'em to think that's a good thing, you idiot."

"All I could think of was how she was completely disrupting my life." And how much he wanted her to continue.

"Uh-huh."

"I didn't ask for her to do that. I didn't ask for her to twine herself around my mind like a ball of silly string until I can't think of anything else. I didn't ask her to come butting in."

"Women," his brother agreed, with a completely understanding sympathetic look on his face. "They're a real dilemma. Just when you think you understand 'em, they do a 180 on you. I spent the week when I'd met Brigit in Paris dizzy as hell."

"Whaddaya do about it?"

Harrison pulled on his earlobe. "First you gotta ask yourself the million-dollar question. Do you love her?"

Sin avoided his brother's eyes. "I don't know. I think about her differently than any woman I've ever known."

"Yep."

"She makes me hurt. Not just my body, but my mind. She kinda gets into my brain somehow so even when I'm not seeing her, I'm seeing her." Scratching his head, Sin sent his brother a quizzical look. "Does that make sense?"

"Unfortunately, it does."

"If I could just get my hands on her, I'd…"

"You'd?"

Tell her how much I love her. Stunned, Sin stared at Harrison. "Oh, my God. I think I'm in love with her. Either that or what happened last night was the most incredible sex I've ever had. Do you think that could be it?"

"It's a thought. But probably too easy."

"Easy," Sin grinned, "was something it definitely wasn't." He could still feel her moving against him, still smell her perfume, feel her mouth on him.

"So what do you think, Sin?"

Sin brought his attention back to his brother. "I think I'm going down for the count and my life is going to be completely turned upside down."

"Yeah, that's what I think, too. It's what happened to me. I had no intention of marrying anyone, much less Brigit. She kept worming her way under my skin until she'd infected me."

Sin wrinkled his nose. "Ahhh…that's appealing."

Grinning in response, Harrison said, "It can be. Think of it as germ warfare. So, when are you going to tell Chastity?"

"Tell her? After last night, she doesn't want anything to do with me." Sin couldn't believe how inept he'd been. How he must have hurt her because he was thrown by his feelings, because he was terrified at the way his life would change by including her.

"You're not going to let that stop you, are you? 'Cause if you are, you aren't any brother of mine."

"Maybe I should take it easy and let her come around in her own time, then I can—"

"Not a good idea. If we left it up to women, Sin, the world wouldn't go anywhere. If you want her, go get her. Drag her by the hair if necessary."

Sin lifted a quizzical brow. "Is that what you did with Brigit?"

With a sheepish expression on his face, Harrison rubbed his nose. "Are you nuts? She might be little, but damn, she's mean."

Sin laughed. "Wimp! Why the hell am I asking you for advice?"

"'Cause I'm your big brother."

"I've usually found that more of a pain than anything else."

"I know, but we're stuck with it."

"Guess so," Sin said. They stared at each other for a moment acknowledging the deep bond that lay between them, even when they annoyed the hell out of each other.

Finally Harrison said, "Bottom line—do you love her? Do you need her?"

"Yeah, I need her. I didn't want to, but I do."

"Then you have to make up your mind to go get her."

Sin thought about it for a few minutes. His brother was right. Now to find the best way to get under her skin. He snapped his fingers as inspiration struck. "What's the florist's name? The one handling the wedding?"

"Rupert. Why?"

"I need to have about ten dozen roses delivered tomorrow before the wedding." He'd woo the woman, until she could think of nothing but him. Just as he could think of nothing but her.

"If you tell Rupert who's calling, he'll probably deliver the flowers himself. You made quite an impression on the poor boy."

"I aim to make an even better impression on Chastity." Damn, this time he'd do it right if it killed him!

THE NEXT AFTERNOON was perfect for a wedding. It had cooled off a bit overnight, but the sun still shone as bright and merry as the musicians leading the wedding procession. The sky was a brilliant blue, accented with billowing white clouds. The perfect clouds for finding cloud pictures, Chastity thought, looking up at them. Smiling, she found a rabbit, a truck and…a puffy heart-shaped image. What a great omen.

She turned her attention to the wedding party. She needed to make sure all costumes were worn correctly, that all flowers were appropriately placed in the hair of the ladies-in-waiting, and the groomsmen were correctly appointed with the right accessories. Satisfied, she marched to the front of the wedding procession, running her experienced eyes one more time over the wedding party. So far, so good. In the ladies' line, Brigit was glowing, attired in a blue gown no less vivid than the sky, with pearls and white roses for accent. Chastity looked to the left. On the men's side, Harrison matched Brigit's elegance in a purple, black, silver and jeweled outfit that shouted of a celebration.

Chastity had tried to avoid looking at Sin, just behind his brother. But there was no way she could keep her eyes from straying in his direction. Every time she looked at him, his gaze was boldly waiting to capture hers. Sin stood at his ease in his wine tunic brightened by gold-and-black tights. Chastity's mouth watered. Sin was the consummate courtier, his dark coloring set off by the rich fabric and short cape, his body emphasized by the close-fitting costume. He caught her looking at him, smiled and blew her a kiss.

Chastity did a double take. Confused, she stared at him. What was he doing? Didn't he remember what happened two days ago? If he did, he wasn't showing it, not the way he did at the rehearsal when he had pretended she didn't exist. Maybe he'd changed his mind.

Seeing him, she wanted him more than ever. She was determined to get him, too, as soon as she figured out how. Before she could make a move toward him, the pipers and drummers began to play and move forward. Hastily, Chastity took her place with the ladies as the two lines wended their way to the chapel.

The wedding party marched around the festival, then finally reached the Tudor-style open-air building in a flourish of bagpipes. The guests were waiting inside, attired in everything from period costumes to shorts and tank tops. The two lines joined at the entrance of the church and waited for the wedding song to begin, before falling into step side by side. Just as they'd rehearsed, richly dressed men and women proceeded to the altar, where Reverend Goodwin waited in his black robes draped with the purple symbols of his profession. The melody changed to the haunting tune of "Greensleeves," which hung in the air in preparation for the bride and groom. Chastity stole a look at Sin from under her lashes as they walked the aisle together. He looked so rakishly handsome that Chastity's breath caught in her throat.

What if this was our wedding? The thought unnerved her so much that she stumbled, bumping into Sin, who immediately placed an arm around her. As she pressed against his side for a moment, she became aware of how right it felt to be there. She looked up to see his face coming closer to hers.

His lips brushed her ear as he whispered, "Hold up there, darlin'. I don't want to lose you."

Surprised at the comment, Chastity snapped out in a terse whisper, "You should have thought about that before, don't you think?"

"I have thought about it. I've thought of nothing but, and I've decided I'm not going to let it happen." Before Chastity could say a word, Sin released her and took his place beside Harrison as Chastity stepped to Brigit's side.

She could scarcely pay attention to the ceremony, so disconcerted was she by Sin's comments. Briefly Chastity noted the lighting of the two candles that combined to make one flame, the exchanging of the vows and the rings and her father's smooth voice as he pronounced Harrison and Brigit, man and wife.

All she was really aware of was Sin.

She'd approach him after the ceremony, Chastity decided. She'd stroll casually over to his side at the reception and ask to speak with him. Then she'd logically explain that she'd been embarrassed and therefore very touchy that night at his house. She'd smile and say, "I wonder if we can start again to see if we might have some type of future relationship." *Future. There's that word again.* She glanced at Sin, who was glancing back. As she met his eyes, Chastity realized that suddenly the future didn't seem so unimportant or threatening. It was real.

"Thank you all for being here on our day of happiness."

Words from the new husband and wife recalled Chastity's concentration to her own duties. Accepting the golden goblet her father handed her, Chastity turned and faced the crowd. With a royal gesture she raised the cup to toast Brigit and Harrison. "And now, may the sun always shine on all of my subjects just as it shines so brightly on this couple joined today. God bless and God speed."

Joyous music filled the air and a tear slipped from her eyes. Brigit and Harrison had looked so happy. She wanted that type of happiness…that over-the-moon giddiness they had shown at the end of the ceremony.

Reverend Goodwin stepped to her side and kissed

her cheek, brushing her tear away. "They're a lovely couple, aren't they?"

Chastity blinked hard, then turned to answer her father. "Yes."

The smile in his eyes deepened. "Don't worry, my dear. Life has big plans for you, too. And so does someone else if I understood it correctly."

Lifting her brows, Chastity said, "Understood what, Father?"

"You'll find out soon enough, Chastity. The curtain's going up and the devil's waiting in the wings. Thank God." With a chuckle he patted her cheek and walked up the aisle and out of the church with the rest of the guests.

It was just like her father to be so enigmatic, Chastity thought, as she watched him stop at the entrance to clasp Sin's arm and exchange a few words. Obviously he knew something she didn't. Not that that surprised her. For a smart woman, she'd been remarkably obtuse. If it weren't for this wedding she might not have seen her future so clearly. A future she now knew she was determined to have with Sin, no matter how difficult it might be. Anything's possible if you work hard enough at it, she thought.

Meeting his eyes as he waited for her near the entrance, Chastity smiled, nerves and excitement competing in her chest. With her heart beating double-time, she walked toward him as fast as her billowing skirt would allow.

Sin swept her a bow. "Your majesty. Your chariot awaits."

"I beg your pardon, sir?"

Tucking her hand into his arm, Sin led her from the chapel. "My trusty steed is at your service."

Chastity wasn't prepared for this approach so she said, somewhat nervously, "You're getting very good at this Renaissance talk and manners." Now if she could only get him to talk in future terms. *Their* future, that was.

"It kind of grows on you, Doc." He grinned down at her. "I'm still not big on the tights, though."

Sin and Chastity emerged into the sunlight to see Brigit and Harrison being pelted with rice before climbing into their open carriage, complete with four horses and liveried driver. Chastity looked around for another vehicle. "Where is this trusty steed of yours?"

Sin pointed at his motorcycle, which was tucked around the other side of the chapel. "Right over there, darlin'."

Chastity's mouth dropped open at the sight. "You're not seriously expecting me to roar up to the reception on a bike?"

"Nope," Sin chuckled.

"Good, 'cause I don't think that's an appropriate way to—"

Sin slipped his arm around her waist. "We're not going to the reception, darlin'."

"What do you mean, we're not— Oh!" Chastity gasped as Sin picked her up and strode toward the bike. "What're you doing?"

Cradling her in his arms, Sin took a firmer hold. "Don't wiggle, I might drop you. I'd hate to see that beautiful gold gown covered with dirt."

Appalled at the amused faces and salacious comments directed at them as they skirted around the crowd, Chastity hissed like an angry cat. "Sin. Put me down. This is embarrassing. My father is right over there. He expects me to do my duty. Not to mention that Brigit and Harrison have expectations."

Sin placed her on the back of the cycle, and climbed on in front of her. "Your father and I have already discussed this."

"Discussed what? You've talked to my father. When?"

"Earlier today, and he was all for what I have planned."

"What do you have— Wait!"

Sin eased the bike forward, glancing back at her. "Tuck up your skirt."

Automatically Chastity gathered the folds of her costume and tucked them under her. Then she righted her crown, which had slipped until it graced her head like a cocked hat on a drunken sailor.

Sin picked up a bit of speed. "Hang on, darlin'."

"Sin. Sin, stop this bike. Let me go." The idiocy of her request suddenly hit her. She grinned as she gripped his waist. Chastity never wanted him to let her go, so what was she fussing about?

"No way." Sin maneuvered carefully around the crowd now following the wedding party's carriage, saying over his shoulder. "Hold on real tight, darlin'. We'll talk about this later."

Chastity sighed and rested her cheek against his shoulder as he left the festival grounds and picked up speed. Perhaps they were going to his house again, she thought, hugging him tighter. It didn't matter. Nothing mattered but that she had him, and she wouldn't let him escape. As the wind rushed through her hair, disarranging her neat upswept hairdo, Chastity realized that she'd go to hell and back with this man if he asked her.

"Sin?"

"What," he called as he turned onto the narrow road that led to the castle grounds.

"Oh, nothing." Chastity smiled as they emerged from the trees. The bright flags were waving gently, as if saying hello and welcome. Her questions could wait. It could all wait—explanations, apologies, all of it.

There was only here and now with the man she loved. She was determined to make the most of it.

Sin pulled into a parking space at the front of the castle, flinging his heels out for balance. He switched off the engine, dismounted and turned to Chastity, reaching to lift her off the seat. For a moment he said nothing, just looked down at her as he held her in his arms. His eyes were so tender, his body so tough as she leaned against him, Chastity thought she'd die from wanting him. Then Sin stepped backward holding her hand, drawing her toward the castle entrance. "Come with me," he whispered.

Chastity's heart was beating so loudly and her breath coming so quickly that she couldn't speak, she could only nod and stumble after him. She followed in silence until they entered the great hall and stood bathed in the jeweled light from the stained-glass windows. Calm descended over her. At least enough so she could glance leisurely around at the recreated history surrounding her before finally opening her mouth to say, "Are you going to show me the past this time, Mr. O'Connor?"

Sin grabbed her hand and gently tugged her over to the stairs. "No, Ms. Goodwin. This time I'm going to show you the present."

Sin started up the staircase, with each set of steps moving faster and faster, climbing higher until they emerged onto the landing outside his room on the third floor where they leaned against the wall, panting like mountain climbers.

"I should have eaten my high-protein cereal this morning," Chastity wheezed, the tight bodice of her costume preventing her from taking very deep breaths.

Sin kissed her forehead. "That's right, you should have, 'cause you're going to need it." He led her across the hall to the closed door of his bedroom. He took her hands in his, gazing deep into her eyes. "This is where it begins."

"Sin," Chastity said, softly, screwing up all of her courage and all of her hope. "Are you trying to tell me something?"

Sin bent down and grazed her lips with his. "I've been trying to tell you something since I first met you. I just didn't know what it was."

"And now you do?"

"Oh, yes," he breathed as he tasted her lips again. "Now I do."

A delicious shiver tickled her spine as she looked at him. "Open the door."

Sin did and Chastity walked into Rapunzel's Bower. The room had changed a bit since she'd last been there with him. It was still draped in lace and light, but now it was also filled with flowers. Flowers in vases on the dresser, strewn on the floor and nestled in the bed coverings. "Oh, Sin, how beautiful." Inhaling, she closed her eyes to better absorb the sweet scent. When she opened them again she focused on the bed and tears filled her eyes. "You've even covered the bed with rose petals."

"When I think of you, I think of flowers." Sin walked up behind her and slipped his arms around her waist, pulling her to him. Chastity leaned her head back onto his chest, sighing as he nuzzled her neck. "I wanted to make love with you among the flowers again. But do it right this time."

Chastity smiled up at him. "I thought you did it pretty good the last time."

Sin's hand cupped her chin, turning her face up for a long, hot kiss. "Not at the end, darlin'."

Chastity turned, linking her arms around his neck. "I didn't do so well, either, Sin. After the way we made love. I mean the way I let myself go with you. I've never done that before." Her heart pounded at the memory. "I felt so awkward. I didn't know what to say, what to do."

"Me, either. After the most incredible experience of my life, I acted like a virgin compromised by a hot date." Sin shook his head in self-disgust. "Before I could come to my senses I'd already stuck both feet in my mouth. No wonder you couldn't wait to get away."

Chastity ran her fingers through his hair, thrilling to the feel of it on her fingers. "I was too sensitive."

Sin dropped kisses on her forehead, eyelids, cheeks, eventually working his way around to her lips. "I kicked out like a jackass because I didn't want anything disrupting my life. Especially not a woman."

Chastity gave him a long, hot, wet kiss that made her knees weak. She pulled back to look at him, noticing his dazed expression. "I didn't want to change my life, either."

A grave look came over Sin's face. "How do you feel about that now?"

"How do you feel?" Chastity longed to tell him, but old habits died hard. She still had trouble believing a man like this could—

Stroking her hair back, Sin said, "I don't want to face the future without you, Chastity."

Chastity felt as if she were melting as she looked at his face. "Oh, Sin," she sighed. "The past means nothing to me if you aren't there."

Their lips met again. Senses stirred, bodies strained against each other as they tried to get closer...closer until they became one. When they fought their way back from the edge of desire they said simultaneously:

"Marry me."

"Will you marry me?"

Chastity tried to focus on the man who held her so firmly. "Say that again. What did you say?"

Sin's wicked smile set Chastity's blood singing. "Let's get in bed and discuss it." He picked her up and laid her back on the rose petals, carefully lying beside her.

"Sin, did you say marry me?"

"I did. Didn't you?"

Chastity nodded. "I did."

Sin laughed. "You know, Doc, this might be the only time in our life we'll ever agree on something."

They both laughed, the laughter falling silent as they met each other's eyes. Chastity ran her hands over his chest, pulling him closer. "I love you."

"And I love you, darlin'." For a long moment there was silence as Sin started to show her how much. In between kisses he said, "It won't be easy, though…working out our lives, but we'll manage it somehow. It's going to be a question of logistics."

"And compromise," Chastity agreed. "But yes, we'll do it."

Sin chuckled. "How about that? We agreed on that, too. Maybe we're making progress."

Chastity slid her hands down over his tights, her fingers searching for the modesty fold in the front. "I know one more thing we can agree on."

Sin nipped her lips, then inhaled sharply as her fingers found him. "What's that?"

Chastity stroked him until he moaned. "These tights have got to go."

Sin slipped his hands under her dress and headed north, not stopping until he reached his target. He leaned down to run his tongue over the top of her breasts, dipping down into the deep valley between. He lifted his head and grinned at her.

"You won't get an argument from me, Doc."

If you enjoyed what you just read,
then we've got an offer you can't resist!

Take 2 bestselling
love stories FREE!
Plus get a FREE surprise gift!

Clip this page and mail it to Harlequin Reader Service®

IN U.S.A.
3010 Walden Ave.
P.O. Box 1867
Buffalo, N.Y. 14240-1867

IN CANADA
P.O. Box 609
Fort Erie, Ontario
L2A 5X3

YES! Please send me 2 free Harlequin Temptation® novels and my free surprise gift. Then send me 4 brand-new novels every month, which I will receive months before they're available in stores. In the U.S.A., bill me at the bargain price of $3.12 plus 25¢ delivery per book and applicable sales tax, if any*. In Canada, bill me at the bargain price of $3.57 plus 25¢ delivery per book and applicable taxes**. That's the complete price and a savings of over 10% off the cover prices—what a great deal! I understand that accepting the 2 free books and gift places me under no obligation ever to buy any books. I can always return a shipment and cancel at any time. Even if I never buy another book from Harlequin, the 2 free books and gift are mine to keep forever. So why not take us up on our invitation. You'll be glad you did!

142 HEN CNEV
342 HEN CNEW

Name	(PLEASE PRINT)	
Address	Apt.#	
City	State/Prov.	Zip/Postal Code

* Terms and prices subject to change without notice. Sales tax applicable in N.Y.
** Canadian residents will be charged applicable provincial taxes and GST.
  All orders subject to approval. Offer limited to one per household.
® are registered trademarks of Harlequin Enterprises Limited.

TEMP99   ©1998 Harlequin Enterprises Limited

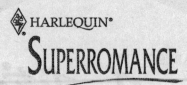